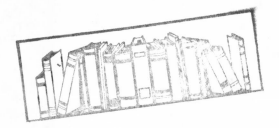

First Hit
of the Season

By Jane Dentinger

FIRST HIT OF THE SEASON
MURDER ON CUE

First Hit
of the Season

JANE DENTINGER

PUBLISHED FOR THE CRIME CLUB BY
DOUBLEDAY & COMPANY, INC.
GARDEN CITY, NEW YORK
1984

F

All of the characters in this book
are fictitious, and any resemblance
to actual persons, living or dead,
is purely coincidental.

2

Library of Congress Cataloging in Publication Data

Dentinger, Jane.
First hit of the season.

I. Title.
PS3554.E587F5   1984   813'.54
ISBN 0-385-19409-9

Library of Congress Catalog Card Number: 83-20700

First Edition

REGIONAL

For my uncle, Clarence Dentinger
1897–1983

I would like to thank all the valued players who performed "fifth business": Dr. Russell Mankes, Dr. Peter Chubinsky, Dr. Mark Dentinger, Dr. Tom Martin, Carol Brener, William L. DeAndrea, Helen and Dick Simon, and Steve Alpert.

First Hit
of the Season

CHAPTER I

Metropolitan Magazine
February 11, 1983

GARBLED GABLER

In an uncertain life, there are several things that I can bank on. Amongst them are death and taxes, a sanitation workers' strike during the hottest week of summer and the certitude that each new theatre season will offer at least one revival of Ibsen's *Hedda Gabler*. This year the honors have been done by the Above Boards Theatre, an Off-Broadway company that has shown great promise of late, under the astute direction of Franklin Allen. And, indeed, Mr. Allen's *Hedda* makes enormous promises but welches on all of them in the end.

Allen's direction is not the culprit here; his staging is fine and flowing and manages to draw the maximum of ironic humor from a dark text in some cleverly pointed scenes. Neither can fault be found with Pia Zeldon's set, nor Marc Carson's lighting, both of which contrive successfully to suggest space and alienation, color and confinement. The supporting cast is uniformly fine, especially David Lassiter's sensually neurotic Lövborg and Keith Thomas's perversely benign Tesman.

What forfeits this production to a confined doom is the casting of Irene Ingersoll in the title role. Miss Ingersoll, who pleased some in recent pieces at the Public, may be of Nordic extraction but her rendering (or should I say rending?) of Hedda is pure Great Neck. Several years too old for the part—which even Carson's cosmeticized lighting can't conceal—Ingersoll supplants the banked fires of Hedda's sexual repression with premenopausal angst. The only convincing thing in her performance is the suggestion of Hedda's pregnancy, thanks to twenty-odd pounds of excess adipose tissue, which is the bulk of Miss Ingersoll's contribution to the play . . . and I do mean *bulk.*

"A *bad* day at Black Rock."

Jocelyn O'Roarke slugged down the rest of her orange juice and Perrier, reached for the telephone and slowly dialed Irene Ingersoll's number. Several unanswered rings gave her faint hope that no one was home and that this "mercy" call could be avoided or at least postponed, but a pick up at the other end killed her craven fantasy. A masculine voice answered.

"Hello—and this better be good."

"Well, better than a poke in the eye with a sharp stick, I guess. Marc, it's Jocelyn, is Irene there?"

"Yeah, just barely. You read Saylin's review?"

"Uh-huh. Fortunately I had breakfast first. How's she doing?"

"Not so hot, Josh. She's a little plastered, to tell the truth."

"God, Marc, it's only ten-thirty!"

"I know, I know. I couldn't stop her. She got the review two hours ago and proceeded to breakfast on pale yellow screwdrivers. What can I tell you?"

"Well, does she want to talk? If not, I can call back later."

"No, don't do that. Hold on a sec' and I'll see if she's up to it."

Marc Carson set down the receiver and went in search of Irene while Jocelyn seethed at the other end and lit a verboten morning cigarette. It wasn't bad enough that Saylin had massacred Irene's performance but he had to go that petty step further and gibe at Irene's relationship with a younger man with that cutting "cosmetic lighting" line, knowing full well that he was delivering a karate chop to a sore point. Jason Saylin's trouble was and had always been that he didn't know where professional critiquing left off and personal trashing began. Jocelyn's ruminations were ended by the clunk of the phone hitting the floor and being clumsily retrieved, followed by an unmistakably distinctive voice, low and mellifluously husky, slurring out a line of seaworthy profanities.

"That walking asshole! Who the hell does he think he is?"

"Irene, you know what they say—those who can do. Those who can't *critique.* Besides . . ."

"Little shit-eating, misogynist faggot. Hell no! He doesn't even have the good taste to be a faggot. He screws women . . . boy, does he ever! Engaged to that anemic little Southern belle, right? Why the hell doesn't he restrict his 'golden showers' to her? Ol' Courtney probably loves 'em. I, however, am not enthused, ya know?"

At this point Irene's tirade ran out of steam and Jocelyn could hear the sound of muffled sobbing through the wires.

Jocelyn said gently, "Irene, it's just one snide man's opinion. The other reviews were . . ."

"The other reviews don't *count*—not as much! Hell, Josh, you know that. And we were hoping to move this one to Broadway. I wanted it so much for Marc and . . . oh, shit, shit. What am I going to do?"

More muffled sobs. Jocelyn stubbed out her cigarette and prepared to administer the "cold splash," a technique she'd newly evolved while coaching actors; it consisted of equal parts positive reinforcement and the harsh facts of show business.

"Okay, I'll tell you what you're going to do. You're going to that theatre tonight and giving the same performance that you've been giving—which is fresh, ferocious and riveting. And you are going to behave as if nothing's happened—unless you want Saylin to win— because you know, if you want this show to move, the most important factors are word-of-mouth and box office. The word-of-mouth is currently fantastic. Hell, Mike Nichols was there last time I saw the show! And your box office is growing nightly. *Hedda* can go to Broadway with this kind of momentum. And if it does, Jason Saylin will have second thoughts about dumping on it twice. It would make him look like the jerk that he is."

There was a breathy pause. "You think so?"

"You bet I do."

"Josh, I'm afraid."

"Who isn't? It's a scary business. What do you want?"

"My mommy," Irene replied, with a short, embarrassed laugh that told Jocelyn that she was revealing a simple truth.

"That I can't supply, but how about a swim at my club on Monday and I'll blow you to lunch at the Gardenia after?"

"Josh, that would be grand, but don't feel you have to . . ."

"Of course I have to. I'm working on my maternal merit badge for Girl Scouts. You want to see me make Eagle, don't you?"

"That's for Boy Scouts."

"Screw you! Then I'll make Lamed Dove. Okay?"

"Okay. See you Monday."

Thus it came to pass that Jocelyn O'Roarke, actress, director and sometimes drama coach, came to be one of the few within the New York theatrical circle to actually witness what was later referred to as the infamous Fettucine Fiasco.

Jocelyn's health club was situated inside Manhattan Plaza, a block-wide, federally funded housing project on Forty-third Street between Ninth and Tenth, reserved solely for the sheltering of the underprivileged—in this case, actors and other hard-working yet frequently unemployed members of the theatrical community. Manhattan Plaza, in the few years since its construction, had made a huge and beneficial impact on this Hell's Kitchen section of New York. It provided a blessed alternative to the starving-in-attics type of actor by setting monthly rents in accordance with the individual tenant's income. Theoretically, Jocelyn thought the Plaza was a noble enterprise; emotionally, she felt it preferable to walk barefoot over burning coals than to come home each night to an elevator full of fellow thespians discussing agents, acting classes and what roles "I've been submitted for." Her gut feeling was that actors are not meant to live in close proximity and that low rents could be a seductive inverse incentive for those neurotic talents, which the theatre is chock full of, who are all too comfortable with failure.

However, she loved the health club, which had the best swimming pool in New York. Even more, she loved the fact that after doing her virtuous fifty-four laps she could run up one flight of stairs to the Gardenia Club, a small and cozily intimate restaurant, and stuff herself with ceviche and great pasta. The fact that Irene and Marc shared a large one-bedroom apartment on the fifteenth floor of the complex made it the ideal rendezvous.

Irene Ingersoll was waiting for her in the club lobby. Despite the fact that she had known Irene well for over eight years and known her in all her infinite variety—commanding and regal onstage, maudlin and in her cups in a West Side bar, bitchy and magnanimous with her intimates—Jocelyn never failed to be a little awe-struck at each encounter. Prone to one of those silly biases, Jocelyn had always thought blond women a little anemic and "lightweight" until she'd met Irene, whose five-foot ten-inch frame, ash-blond hair and sell-your-soul-to-have-it bone structure reordered her conceptions. Heavy or slender—and Irene's weight did tend to fluctuate—she was one of the most sensual, vital and intelligent women that Jocelyn had ever met. She could also be a monumental pain in the ass, as Jocelyn had discovered when she directed her in a workshop production of *Mother Courage*, but her ferocious dedication and irreverent humor made her worth the trouble.

"Aha! O'Roarke, I've got one for you. What did the leper say to the prostitute?"

"Keep the tip."

"Oh shit! You're no fun. Let's go swim."

Glad to see that her friend was not in a brooding mood, Jocelyn quickly assented and was soon doing her fifty-four hard laps alongside Irene's leisurely breaststrokes—the perfect juxtaposition of athletics and élan. Jocelyn emerged wet and the trimmer of the two but was fully aware that the gaze of every poolside man was firmly fixed on Irene's undulating return to the showers.

Forty-five minutes later two glowingly healthy and well-groomed actresses sat across from each other in the Gardenia Club, sipping white wine and perusing their menus. Irene shot Jocelyn a wicked grin.

"Eh, O'Roarke, we look pretty damn spiffy, *n'est-ce pas?*"

"Indeed, we do . . . and we damn well better!"

"God, yes. I love living here, but when I lived down in the Village I used to schlep around the neighborhood all day in jeans, a work shirt and no makeup. Here, I can't even go out to get the paper in the morning without getting duded up. I mean, what if Tennessee Williams got in the elevator! Then I'd never get to play Blanche."

"Don't worry, I'll put in a good word for you," Jocelyn said nonchalantly while lighting a cigarette. Irene raised an incredulous eyebrow.

"Are you serious or did you stay in the sauna too long?"

Jocelyn laughed. "I did have drinks with him . . . here, as a matter of fact. I was celebrating my emancipation from my old agent, Albert 'The Albatross' Carnelli, with a few friends and a lot of champagne and Williams was by himself at the bar, so I invited him to join us."

"And he *did?!*"

"Sure he did. He's a sweet man and, given enough champagne, I'm damned irresistible."

"What did you talk about?"

"Well, it was slow going at first. Everybody was appalled by my cheek and a little awestruck. But he and I got into a long, earnest conversation about the best way to keep your goggles from fogging up in the pool. He'd been having trouble with his, you see, and I told him that a little spit in the lenses would do the trick every time. He seemed to think that was very funny, for some reason."

Slowly Irene said, "You talked to Tennessee Williams about *spitting* on goggles?"

"Yeah, that's right. Works, too."

"Jocelyn, I know you are very gifted in your chosen field, but are you sure you wouldn't be happier as a gym instructress?"

"Could be. Let's order. I'm starved."

It was shaping up to be a better luncheon than Jocelyn had expected. Irene made no mention of Saylin's devastating review. Instead, she flirted outrageously with the young waiter, who had seen her Hedda the week before and was gratifyingly enthralled, and gossiped about all their mutual acquaintances who had come to the show. Jocelyn had just savored her first bite of a delicious crabmeat salad and was about to ask Irene for a taste of her fettucine when she spied, over Irene's shoulder, the only sight in the world capable of killing her appetite at that moment—Jason Saylin entering the dining room with his fiancée, Courtney Mason, a lithe and stunning redhead. This was doubly bad, for Jocelyn knew Courtney, a sometime actress, from a show they had done together five years ago. Even if Jocelyn could keep Irene from noticing Saylin, could she also keep Courtney from noticing her? Courtney came from Georgia and was a Southern belle of the old school. If she sighted Jocelyn, her sense of noblesse oblige, or noblesse of bilge, as Jocelyn thought of it, would demand that she come over to "say hey."

Jocelyn ducked her head and took a large sip of Chablis before she realized that Irene was asking her a question.

"So what's up with him?"

"Hmm? Him who?"

"Him who! Your knight in shining armor, you nit. That detective fellow, Gerrard, who helped you get your neck out of a noose when Harriet Weldon was killed. Does that ring a bell?"

"Oh, Phillip, yeah."

"Don't you 'oh, Phillip, yeah' me, missy. And don't you try to hold out on me, either. I keep my ear clued to the grapevine and word has it that Rocky O'Roarke had finally fallen down the well, but good. Hell, you dropped Kevin Kern for this guy. He must be *something!* So tell."

She did not want to talk about Phillip Gerrard, especially at this moment. But, if it would keep Irene diverted, she had little choice.

"We still see each other."

Irene's elegantly arched eyebrow conveyed infinite derision.

"Well, how nice. How civil. Means *nothing!* Come on, Josh, *give!*"

Distraught, Jocelyn snapped, "There's nothing to give, Irene! He's not someone you can summarize easily. And it's not a relationship that's easy to describe. Hell, it's not an easy relationship, period."

Irene said patiently, "Jocelyn, as long as I've known you, there's always been one topic on which you are infinitely articulate and that is—men. You'll have to do better than this."

"Alright, alright. Phillip is . . . a lot of the things that I've always looked for in a man. He's smart and funny and insightful . . . and *not* an actor. He's extremely good at what he does and he cares about it, as much as I care about what I do, which is . . . great."

"Gotcha. And there's something un-great behind that 'great.' What is it?"

"Oh shit, it sounds so clichéd! We live in two different worlds. I deal in 'what if' and he deals in 'what is.' I like to go to bed at three and he has to be up by seven. When he's on a tough case, I won't see him for days on end. Then we arrange to meet for dinner, and I'm caught up with how to get a laugh at the end of act two and he's thinking about the body of a battered child that he saw that morning. So he's tired and doesn't want to hear about the laugh in act two and I'm all keyed up and, frankly, can't bear to hear about the dead child because it's too awful, and I'm a coward. Then I feel guilty and he feels depressed. And that's what's not great."

"But do you love him?"

Jocelyn laughed sadly. This conversation and her own unexpected outpourings had almost taken her mind off the couple sitting behind them.

"Oh, Irenie, fairy princess, that is not the penultimate question. I respect Phillip and care for him . . . I quite possibly do love him. The real question is, Am I *good* for him? Most times, lately, I feel like I'm not."

Irene looked thoughtfully at the piece of pasta that she was gracefully twirling around her fork before replying. "You know, Josh, I'm not a great one for telling people what to do. But, in this one case, I'd just like to say—"

Whatever it was that Irene was about to say Jocelyn never found out. At that instant an uproarious laugh broke out from the neighboring table. Irene jerked her head around and saw her nemesis sitting behind her. What was worse, she heard him.

"I'm *not* exaggerating, Courtney. They should've called it *Hedda, Dearest.* Ingersoll has no finesse. It was just two hours of watching a Nordic cow in heat—*udder*-ly depressing! Just once, I'd like to see a show cast on merit alone. The only reason Irene's playing Hedda is because Franklin Allen has a yen for her little playfellow, Carson. Now, there *must* be an easier way to seduce the boy. Allen could've just waited for Irene to get even fatter."

It was a moment that Jocelyn would forever remember in slow motion—the languid toss of Saylin's head, the abrupt catch of breath as Courtney's glance met hers and the deep timber of Irene's voice, which seemed to come from far away. "Well, that tears it."

In one fluid movement Irene Ingersoll rose with fettucine in hand and turned to the table behind her.

"Mr. Saylin," her voice cracked like a whip above the patrons' heads, "you can say what you like about me in print, that's your privilege. But, when you dump on me in public, I dump back—get it?"

With a deft twist of the wrist Irene deposited the rest of her fettucine on Jason Saylin's gleaming head and strode serenely out of the dining room. Jocelyn threw money down on the table and dashed after her friend, trying her best to ignore Courtney's beseeching gaze and the spectacle of New York's most famous critic wiping cream sauce out of his eyes.

CHAPTER II

"Your hair's on fire."

"Hmm . . ."

Phillip Gerrard stared perplexedly at the crown of Jocelyn's head and speared a thick slice of Nova Scotia salmon. For the past twenty minutes she had been riveted on the same page of *Metro Magazine,* and all his efforts to distract her had been for naught. It was time for drastic measures.

"Josh, I think I should tell you . . . I'm seeing someone else."

"You're *what?*"

He was very gratified to see her head snap up and the dangerous gold glint in her hazel eyes. Sunday brunch at Jocelyn O'Roarke's apartment was one of the high points of his week and he saw no reason why he should be upstaged by a magazine article.

"Ah, ah. Put down that butter knife, please. I was just kidding."

"Well, it's a little early in the day for quaint humor, Gerrard." She buttered a croissant with feigned nonchalance and waited for the wave of jealous anger to ebb. After years of laissez-faire relationships she was deeply unnerved to discover that when she really cared for someone, as she did for this man, she was a very jealous woman. Feeling calmer, she raised her eyes to meet his. His black hair was rumpled, he hadn't shaved yet and he was wearing the velour bathrobe she had given him for Christmas, along with a very self-satisfied smile. She promptly threw her croissant at him. He caught it in his left hand and laughed.

"Well, I'm glad one of us is having a good time. *Damn* you, Phillip!"

He tossed the mangled croissant back onto her plate and caught her hand in his. "Easy, old girl. It was just tit for tat. I'd just like to know what piece of tawdry print could distract you so long from the man who loves you, eh?"

She returned his smile and felt herself blush, which was ridiculous. You are not supposed to blush after you hit thirty, but she did every time Phillip told her that he loved her. Ridiculous.

"Tawdry is the operative word, alright," she said, tossing the magazine his way. "It's Jason Saylin's monthly column. Read it and retch."

Gerrard picked up *Metro Magazine*. He was familiar with the column titled "Saylin's Solution," which didn't consist of reviews, but rather the author's thoughts about the "state of the art" and whatever juicy pieces of backstage gossip he could work into it. Halfway down the page he spotted the source of Jocelyn's preoccupation.

Due to recent events, this writer is seriously considering a petition to Lloyd's of London in favor of a new insurance clause covering "actor attacks." If Angie Dickinson can insure her legs, I would at least like the option of insuring my person and wardrobe from the assault of addled actresses whose egos are bigger than their talent and even their body mass. So my advice to a certain het up Hedda is: Go easy on the cocktails and, if you can't take the heat, stay out of the spotlight.

Now it was his turn to be preoccupied but Jocelyn, who had less patience than he, began an aggressive game of footsies under the table. "So what do you think?"

"Huh? Well . . . I think he's gotten better."

"What?"

"As a writer, I mean . . . Oh, look it's a very snide piece and I'm sorry about your friend and the trouble she's let herself in for. It's just that, whenever I read his stuff, I'm always amazed that it's as good as it is. I never expect it of him; it wasn't particularly his strong suit in college."

"In college?! I seemed to have missed a chapter here. Phillip, are you saying you went to college with *Jason Saylin?"*

"Yeah, only for a year, though. He was a senior when I was a freshman at Northwestern. And don't look so apoplexed—I wasn't always a cop, you know."

"But, my God, Jason Saylin! Why on earth didn't you tell me?"

"Because we had more pressing matters to discuss," he replied with an insinuating grin, "and I didn't know him all that well. His name wasn't Saylin back then. It was Drucker—Ainsly Drucker. He was in the theatre department, of course. Started out as an actor, a pretty bad one, then switched gears to directing. I remember that whenever I'd see him in the student union he'd be holding court with a half-dozen comely coeds and tossing around names like Artaud and Grotowski. He wrote a little for the school paper, nothing memorable. But his main love was play writing. The department even produced a Drucker original, directed by the author, of course. I think it was called *The Age of Angst,* or maybe I'm just remembering what sitting through it felt like. It was a real dog. I always thought his pal Andre would become the writer."

Jocelyn gagged on her croissant, "You mean Andre Guérisseur was there, too?"

"Sure. We used to call them Famous and Andy. I knew Andre a little better. We worked on the paper together. He was a very shy guy who kept to himself, mostly because of his stuttering problem, I guess. But he was smart as a whip and one hell of an editor. Funny how things turned out."

"I'll say. Old school chums, eh? You'll have to give me a moment here while my mind boggles."

And boggle it did. Everyone who knew Jason Saylin knew Andre Guérisseur, the same way that everyone who knew Robinson Crusoe knew Friday. Guérisseur was Saylin's secretary and general aide-de-camp. In the theatre community he was referred to by a variety of nicknames, among them "The Shadow," "God's Right Hand" and, by the less kind, "Igor." Jocelyn couldn't recall a single opening night that Saylin had attended without the silent, hunched figure of Guérisseur by his side, every inch the good and faithful servant, but certainly not the *friend!*

Jocelyn poured them both a second cup of coffee and asked, "How the devil did those two hook up, Phillip?"

Gerrard shook his head and smiled ruefully at Jocelyn. He understood her well enough to know that she was after more than just gossip. Like all good actors she had a boundless curiosity about the how and why of human relationships. But she could go on like this for hours and he had his own amorous plans on the agenda.

"I don't really know, love. Maybe it was just the old story about opposites attracting . . . or maybe they each had something the other one wanted."

"Like what?"

"Well, to put it simply—and this is all speculation, mind you—I think Saylin wished he had Andre's brains and I think Andre wished he had Saylin's . . . girls."

"You're kidding?"

"Nope. Guérisseur had a real eye for the ladies . . . and Ol' Jason had a real way with them. So just chalk it up to symbiosis."

"Hmm, I guess. They do say that vicarious thrills are the best ones."

"Then they lie."

Jocelyn cocked her head and smiled. "You think so, Mr. Gerrard?"

"I know so, Miss O'Roarke."

In this way they proceeded from the general to the particular, and ten minutes later Phillip was well on the way to completing his agenda when the phone started ringing.

"Damn! I forgot to unplug the phone."

Phillip grabbed her hand and whispered, "Let it ring."

"I can't," she groaned. "If I don't hear it, I'm fine. But when I do, I'm like Pavlov's dog—I have to answer."

With all her heart, not to mention her libido, Jocelyn prayed that it would be a brief call—Channel Thirteen fund raising or something equally simple to deal with. Hearing the voice at the other end, she sighed and abandoned habitation of the Place of Hope.

"Did you read that son of a bitch's column? Christ! I could kill him."

"Yes, Irene, I saw it. Take it easy, now."

At the mention of Irene's name Gerrard raised his head from the sofa cushions and shot her a look that was equal parts ireful and resigned. Instinctively his hand reached down to pick up the sports page.

"That bastard's not going to get away with this."

"Look, Irene, there's nothing you can do about—"

"Oh, yes there is, Josh. There *is* something I can do. I can fight fire with fire. And, believe me, it's gonna be one hell of a conflagration!"

"What are you talking about?"

"Like I said before, sweetie, if he wants to dump garbage I can dump it right back. A certain friend of mine—an actor who's down on his luck—he deals a little."

"Deals what?"

"Coke, angel, and not the Joan Crawford kind . . . just to help pay the rent, you know? Nothing big, but he knows people. Anyway, he's given me some inside news. Not only does Jason Saylin have a big stick up his ass, he has an even bigger straw up his nose! How do you like that?"

"Not much," Jocelyn said wearily, "but it's not such a big deal, Irene. It's a fad with the nouveau riche. Like Robin Williams said, 'Cocaine is God's way of telling you you're making too much money.' And who cares?"

"Oh, I think *Metro Magazine* and a certain New York newspaper will care when they hear that he toots to the tune of five hundred bucks a week and is known to snort before each and every opening he attends. I think they'll care a whole hell of a lot."

Seriously worried now, Jocelyn said, "I can't believe that's really true. But, even if it is, Irenie, you don't want to do this!"

"And why the hell not?!"

"Because, for one thing, it will only make matters worse. You could make yourself liable for an ugly law suit, which won't help you or the show. Secondly, it's stooping to his level. And I don't want to see you do that. You don't win that way."

There was a long pause before Irene Ingersoll answered, "No—but I get even."

Jocelyn heard a sharp click at the other end and gingerly replaced the receiver. Seeing the bleak look on her face, Phillip asked, "So what've we got here, O'Roarke?"

"I'll tell you what we've got. We've got trouble in River City."

CHAPTER III

"Tickets, please . . . Just go down the center aisle, ma'am." The towheaded young usher handed Jocelyn her stubs and shot an admiring glance at her maroon crepe dress with the peekaboo V neckline and all that it encompassed. She gave him a dazzling smile and glided past him, mentally flipping the bird to Detective Phillip Gerrard, who had once again stood her up to keep a hot date with a cold corpse. This time, however, he had supplied her with another escort; Sergeant Tommy Zito, his right-hand man, followed in her wake. As they took their seats, she handed Zito his program and tried to gauge his reaction to the pandemonium about him. Broadway opening nights, artistic considerations aside, are brightly burning candles to the media moths of Manhattan. The famous and the infamous come, not just to see but to be seen. Tommy Zito looked about as happy as a vegetarian at a bullfight and ready to burst out of his immaculate dress shirt and rented tux. Adding to his overall discomfort, Jocelyn felt sure, was the fact that he had to spend an evening in her company.

When Zito had first met Jocelyn, she had been a prime suspect in a murder case. The fact that she had been instrumental in finding Harriet Weldon's real killer might have softened his attitude toward her if she had not, in the process, also managed to stake a large claim on the time and attentions of his boss. Jocelyn had a hunch that anything Lassie ever felt for Timmy, Zito felt for Phillip, and for this she liked him enormously . . . if only he didn't make her feel like Bette Davis in *Of Human Bondage*.

"So, Tommy, where's Dick Tracy off to tonight?"

Zito stared uncomprehendingly at his program and muttered, "East Village . . . body in a garage . . . shot through the head. Looks like it's drug related . . . probably a dealer caught skimming."

It was like trying to converse with a teletype, but she pressed on. "Do you think he'll be able to make the party afterwards?"

"He said if he could, he would. So, if he can . . . he will."

"Thus spake Zarathustra."

"Huh?"

She was about to reply when a hand was laid on her arm, and she looked up to see an old actor friend who had recently found favor and big bucks in the land of TV.

"Hey, O'Roarke, lookin' good! When're you coming back to L.A.? We miss you."

"When they fly me first-class, Danny! When did you get to town?"

"Yesterday. I was starting to get depressed by sunshine. And I wanted to see Irenie strut her stuff. She's waited a long time for this. Hey, next time you're in Lotus Land, why don't you stay with me and Rhea?"

"Oh, that's sweet of you. I'd love to."

"Good . . . we got a date, then."

After Danny moved on, Tommy Zito turned an awestruck gaze toward Jocelyn and asked, "You really know that guy?"

"Really and truly."

"I watch him every week. He's on—"

"Yeah, I know. Contain yourself, Thomas. The curtain's going up."

Even when the house went to total black she could still feel Zito's intense stare and smiled to herself, knowing that she had just scored a huge point with the feisty Italian. Now just let him not hate the play, she prayed. She cringed at the idea of having to go backstage and greet Irene on the night of her Broadway opening with a recalcitrant cop in tow. *Hedda Gabler* had finally made it to Broadway and Jocelyn didn't want anything to spoil Irene's evening.

Forty minutes later, her fears were forgotten. After an initial ten minutes of fidgeting, Tommy Zito had become mesmerized as soon as Irene had hit the stage. For all her height and weight she prowled the stage like a beautiful tigress looking for fresh meat. By turns charming then cutting, cold then erotic, she ignited the audience but skillfully kept the fires banked. Jocelyn had never seen her be better. She felt a familiar chill run up her spine, the recognition that she was witnessing an inspired performance, as Irene uttered the second-act curtain line, "And then—at ten o'clock—Eilert Lövborg comes—with vine-leaves in his hair."

As the houselights came up she turned to her companion.

"So, what do you think, Tommy?"

Zito's tie was loose and his hair wet with perspiration.

"Whoa—what a woman! Holy Jeez, I need a drink."

Respectful of the toll that good theatre takes on the uninitiated, Jocelyn gently led Zito out to the lobby bar. No sooner had they gotten their drinks when the onslaught hit.

"Joshie, honey!" a voice caroled behind her. She winced and took another belt of champagne, needing the fortification. Only one person in the world called her by that awful appellation and that was Courtney Mason. She turned with a fixed smile and politic heartiness. "Why, Miss Mason-Dixon, how the hell are you?"

"Just fine, darlin'. And you?" Courtney wafted up to Jocelyn and planted a careful kiss on her cheek. In a black silk off-the-shoulder dress, which made a striking contrast to her milk-white skin and abundant red hair, Courtney made quite an effect. She turned toward Tommy Zito and warmly grabbed his wrist. "Now, don't tell me. You must be Joshie's new beau that I've been hearin' so much about. That mysterious Detective Gerrard person we've all been dyin' to meet."

Tommy flushed beet red and started muttering disclaimers, half in Italian. Jocelyn swiftly intervened and made the proper introductions. Zito was clearly fascinated by Courtney but had little to say, so Jocelyn, having not seen Courtney since the scene in the Gardenia Club, moved on to small talk. One of the good things that could be said about Courtney was that she had the true Southern instinct for avoiding sore points at any cost. No mention was made about Saylin's scathing review of Irene, nor of Irene's retaliatory threats. The tacit agreement between the two women was to let sleeping dogs lie as low as they possibly could. If Irene and Saylin had agreed to bury the hatchet, the least Jocelyn could do was to make herself pleasant to Jason's fiancée.

"I know Jason's around here somewhere, Courtney. But I don't see him."

"Oh, he's mingling with the bigwigs. I swear, I'm lucky if I get that man alone for fifteen minutes at a stretch."

"Well, as long as it's a nice, long stretch," Jocelyn said, demurely sipping her drink. She had never been able to resist giving Courtney a shot when opportunity offered. Three months of playing across from a limited actress, who cared more about who was in the audience than who was onstage with her, had left Jocelyn a little testy. But Courtney also held a certain fascination for her. Coming from a rough-and-tumble childhood with two older brothers who had taught her everything from poker to touch football, Jocelyn had been struck dumb by her first encounter with a genuine magnolia-kissed Southern belle. Southern women are High Priestesses in the Temple of Feminine Charm and the God they serve is Man; however, unlike most acolytes, they have an uncanny knack for making God play by *their* rules. Even coming from a tradition with such high standards, Courtney was no slouch. As someone once said to Jocelyn when Courtney was dating a fast-rising young playwright, "La Mason is the Kissinger of Sex."

Fitting a Virginia Slim into an ebony holder, Courtney raised eyes filled with the breathless hope that Man would make Fire for her. But even as Tommy scrambled madly in his back pocket for a pack of U.S. Auto School matches, a gold Cartier lighter came to her rescue.

"Andre, lamb, aren't you sweet. I didn't even see you there. Meet an old friend of mine, Joshie O'Roarke, and her friend Mr. Zito. Ya'll, this is Andre Guérisseur."

"Pleased to m-meet you, Miss O'Roarke, Mr. Z-Zito."

Jocelyn grasped a limp, cold hand and gazed down at Andre Guérisseur. Stoop-shouldered and balding, he stood protectively at Courtney's delicately boned elbow, and all Jocelyn could think of, despite her best efforts, was the Princess and the Frog. They chatted aimlessly for a few minutes until Guérisseur tapped Courtney gently on the wrist.

"I think we'd better find Jason. You know they a-always remark on it if he isn't in his seat when the act starts."

Courtney graciously murmured her assent and was starting to make fond adieus when Jocelyn broke in. "By the way, Andre, a good friend of mine tells me he was at Northwestern with you—Phillip Gerrard."

A surprisingly attractive smile lit up Guérisseur's face at this piece of news, and what the optimistic would call a twinkle came into his gray eyes. "Now you don't s-say? You know the old F-Flipper, do you?"

"The *what?*"

"The Flipper. I dubbed him that, actually." As Andre warmed to his topic Jocelyn noticed that his stutter all but disappeared. "When we worked on the school paper together he was dating two girls, one a cheerleader and the other a philosophy major. He liked them both equally well—but for very different reasons, I suspect. Anyway, every Friday before we left the office, he'd flip a coin to see which one he'd ask out on Saturday. It was a fascinating ritual."

Tommy's eyes were beginning to bulge, but Jocelyn was hot on the trail.

"I bet it was. Machismo can be so quaint. And that's how he decided, eh?"

"Actually, no. He said what decided him was his reaction to however the toss came out. That told him which one he really wanted to see that weekend. I thought it was a brilliant scheme. Is he anywhere about tonight? I'd l-love to see him."

"Well . . . uh . . . not at the moment." Jocelyn would see herself damned before she'd admit to being stood up in front of Courtney. "But we're meeting him later on."

"W-Wonderful! Tell you what, a group of us are going over to Jason's apartment after the party. I'm sure Jason would like to see Phillip, too. Why don't the three of you drop by?"

"Now, Andre, darlin', don't get all pushy on these people. They probably have plans of their own." There was a faint coolness in Courtney's voice which suggested to Jocelyn that she was less than enchanted by Guérisseur's invitation. She picked up her cue.

"Well, we were really planning on spending the evening with . . . uh . . . Irene."

Andre clapped his hands together. "That's perfect, then. Jason told me that Irene's coming over, too. She can bring all of you with her."

Lacking Courtney's bloodlines, Jocelyn blurted out a strangled, "She *is?!*"

"Oh, yes. Didn't you know?" Andre asked blithely. "Marc and Franklin are coming along, too. Please come. It'll be such f-fun."

Irene's second act was even better than her first, but Jocelyn was having a hard time paying attention. Actresses do not, as a rule, celebrate their opening night with the critics who are going to be reviewing them. And the idea of Irene and Saylin hobnobbing together at an intimate gathering seemed as likely as the Montagues and the Capulets getting together for a Tupperware party. This had to be the work of a third party—some kind of Super Yenta, the likes of which any public relations firm would give its eyeteeth to hire. Jocelyn was still trying to figure out who it could be as she automatically rose to her feet to give Irene a well-deserved ovation.

As Jocelyn gently led a dazed Tommy Zito up the center aisle, she spotted a familiar figure at the back of the auditorium and felt a warm glow start in the pit of her stomach. In a charcoal gray suit that went well with his jet-black hair and Tyrone Power eyebrows, Phillip could have passed for a successful actor or an affluent producer, but no one would cast him as a hard-working cop. It amazed her now to remember that when she had first met him that was all she saw—the cop, not the man.

Wearing a devilish grin, he patted Zito on the shoulder before slipping his arm comfortably around Jocelyn's waist. "So, Thomas, what d'ya make of all of this? Frankly, sport, you look like you've been hit with a brick."

Tommy shook his head, trying to regain some kind of equilibrium. "Phil . . . I don't know, I tell ya! She's one fantastic broad, that Ingersoll. It was like . . . like watching Aaron Pryor go in for the kill! Only she's taller . . . but I tell ya, if she'd been born a guy, she'd a made a great boxer. No lie."

Gerrard threw his head back and laughed raucously until Jocelyn kicked his ankle. Seeing Tommy's evident dismay, he said contritely, "Sorry, Tommy. You're dead on the money. I saw most of the last act. She's a champ, alright." Turning to Jocelyn, he asked, "Happy, Mother Hen? Your chick did good."

"Yeah, she did. But I have a funny feeling that the play's not over."

"What does that mean?"

"That means that we're going to a party where The Champ may well see fit to throw a few more punches. So hold on to your hat and follow me . . . Flipper."

Phillip Gerrard's jaw dropped open as Tommy uttered one huge "Ha!" and Jocelyn swept past both men out to the lobby.

CHAPTER IV

"Would you kindly, kindly tell me just what the hell gives here?"

"Hmm? What, Josh?" Irene Ingersoll, in a flowing forest-green crepe gown and full-length mink, was at her most regal and ethereal best. "Where's that nice Mr. Zito? Isn't he coming?"

"No, he's not. After the number you did on him at the Waldorf —and I must say, for a blonde, your Duse impersonation is great— his blood pressure couldn't take any more. He's probably flying to Rome right now to petition for your canonization."

A feline smile lit Irene's face. "Such a sweet little man . . . You'd never guess he was a pig."

"Irene, stop futzing with me! We don't have the time."

They were riding in an elevator up to Jason Saylin's Central Park West penthouse. It was the first time all evening that Jocelyn had managed to get a moment alone with Irene, and she intended to make the most of it. For a few seconds Irene withstood Jocelyn's relentless gaze, then gave an eloquent shrug and pulled a joint out of her beaded evening bag. She lit it, took a hungry draw and passed it to her friend.

"Goddamn, Josh! You think I like this—having to come here and make nice with that pissant?! It wasn't *my* idea!"

"I didn't think so. Whose was it?"

"Franklin's. I mean, he's the director and I'm just following my blocking. When he found out I wanted to blow the whistle on Jason's coke habit, he nearly had puppies. I should've kept my mouth shut. Franklin Allen is the living, breathing reincarnation of Pollyanna. He wants to be liked by *everybody* . . . but, most especially, by Jason Saylin. Don't ask me why."

Her curiosity finally satisfied, Jocelyn became more philosophical. "Well, you can't really blame him, can you? The Above Boards Theatre Company has been struggling to make it for a long time now, and this is the first production they've managed to move to Broadway. Its success means a lot to Franklin. I guess he figures this little get-together is one way of insuring it."

Irene took a second toke and wrinkled her nose. "Then he should guess again. I mean, I'll play out this little farce if he wants me to. I'll play it to the hilt. But I don't, for a second, think it's going to make any difference as far as Saylin's review goes. If he's still out to get me, he'll get me."

"And what'll you do if he does?"

"Oh, I'll think of something . . . Come on, pet. We're here."

Jason Saylin's apartment was large, luxurious and so art deco you could cut yourself on it—the kind of place Jocelyn loved to prowl around in but was very glad she didn't have to wake up to every morning. They were met at the door by Courtney, who proceeded to go into ecstasies over Irene's dress, leaving Jocelyn free to greet Andre Guérisseur.

"Miss O'Roarke . . . Jocelyn, I'm so glad you could c-come. Is Phillip joining us?"

"Oh, yes. Have no fear. The Flipper is parking his car and should be with us any second now. That's probably him now."

Andre went to answer the door. He made a wide, careful arc around Courtney and Irene, whom he seemed to regard as some kind of reborn Medusa judging by the way he averted his gaze from her direction. He opened the door to not one, but three new arrivals; Phillip stood there, flanked on either side by Franklin Allen and Marc Carson. Together the three of them looked like an ad for men's all-sized fashions, with Franklin measuring five foot three tops, next to Phillip's five nine, which was in turn dwarfed by Carson's rangy six foot one. Blue-eyed with sandy blond hair and an immaculate smile, Marc Carson had for a time been a favorite model at *Gentlemen's Quarterly*, until Irene had encouraged him to follow his talent and inclination and take up lighting design full-time. After shaking hands with Andre, he affectionately greeted Jocelyn with a hug that lifted her three inches off the ground.

"Hey, Rocky! Met your fella in the elevator coming up. He's alright. Better not try any rabbit punches with this one, slugger."

Jocelyn groaned, "Oh, Christ. Marc, you didn't go and tell him the Blarney Stone story, did you?"

Carson grinned and gave her nose a tweak. "Had to, Josh. Code of the Locker Room and all that stuff. Besides, a guy's gotta know what he's up against."

As Carson went to join his lady love, Franklin Allen came up and bussed Jocelyn on the cheek, pausing long enough to whisper in her ear, "My compliments on your taste, Miss O'Roarke. He is to die, Jocelyn, really to die." With that the ginger-haired little man bounced toward the living room as if he had springs on his feet. He was greeted with cheers and whistles, which he acknowledged with a mock bow and a blush that almost obliterated his freckles.

Phillip was still in the foyer with Guérisseur, embroiled in what looked to be an orgy of reminiscence. Jocelyn shrugged and went in search of a drink, thinking that it was too bad and just like Cruel Fate to take the wind out of her "Flipper" sails by acquainting Phillip with the story of her one and only barroom brawl . . . and all in one evening, too, worst luck.

Ten minutes later she had found consolation in a glass of Moët and the vicarious pleasure of watching Irene and Marc savor their triumph. They moved as a unit, majestic and charming, greeting friends, thanking admirers and looking for all the world like the perfect topping on a Swedish wedding cake. Just as a ribald and slightly sodden wit was making a toast to "the Light and her Lighter," Jocelyn was joined by Phillip and Andre, looking as thick as thieves and twice as dangerous. Knowing the ribbing that was in store for her, she launched an immediate counteroffensive.

"Well, hello! I didn't know if I'd ever see you two again. And I'm still not sure if I'll ever see our host . . . Andre, where is Jason? I haven't laid eyes on him yet."

Unwittingly, she had struck a nerve, for Guérisseur actually paled as his eyes whipped around the room. "Isn't he here? Oh . . . well, he must have . . . I think I'd better go fetch him. Be right back."

As Andre scurried off, Phillip ordered a drink and took a long, meditative sip while studying his suddenly silent companion.

"Here I am, alone at last with 'Rocky O'Roarke,' pugilist queen of the Upper West Side. If only Tommy Zito knew . . ."

"Aw, come on, Phillip, give me a break. It was no big deal. Whatever Marc told you, divide by six."

"My math's not so good. Why don't you give me the true equation?"

"Alright, already." Jocelyn leaned against the bar, giving him a wry smile. "Two years ago I was celebrating St. Patrick's Day with Irenie and Marc and some friends. We ended up going to the Blarney Stone on Forty-second and Ninth for corn beef and cabbage. There was an obnoxious drunk there who wouldn't take no for an answer. He tried to corner me when I was coming out of the ladies' room, so I, uh . . ."

"You decked him."

"Well . . . more or less. I didn't *know* he had a glass jaw!"

"Of course not, love," Phillip said soothingly, running a finger gently along the line of Jocelyn's cheek. "Fortunately, I like my women mean and ornery."

Jocelyn bit the finger which stroked her. "Smart ass! No wonder people avoid you in droves. I notice Ol' Jason hasn't beaten a path over here yet."

All playfulness suddenly evaporated as he gazed down at the cream-colored carpet, frowning. "I expect there's several reasons for that."

"Such as?"

"First off, in case you've forgotten, my line of work does tend to make some people uncomfortable . . . especially, assuming what Irene says is true, if they're into coke and have it on the premises. And, of course, it might not be fun for Jason to run into someone who knew him when he was plain old Ainsley Drucker from Galena, Illinois. He might find it embarrassing."

He finished his drink and placed his empty glass on the bar without ever taking his eyes off the rug fibers. She paused a moment to get them both fresh drinks. Studying his profile, she handed him his glass and said quietly, "You know, Phillip, you are *almost* as good an actor as I am a snoop—but not quite! Hell, *lots* of people went to Northwestern with Saylin. I'm sure he's run into quite a few. And the man does not embarrass easily. So, what's the scoop, ducks?"

He looked up at her, shaking his head with a rueful smile. "Damned if you don't take all, Josh."

"All I can get . . . Now give."

"Alright . . . I once saw something happen that Jason would rather I hadn't. Andre once invited me out to dinner with him and Jason. We went to this little Italian place off campus and, while we were having dinner, Jason . . . well, he had a fit."

"Huh? What happened? The waiter bring the wrong wine?"

"No! A *real* fit. Jason had a seizure. He's an epileptic, Josh."

Jocelyn spilled half of her champagne on the carpet, which mercifully was the same shade. "Holy Moses, that *is* news. But Phillip, why . . . I mean it's a pity and I'm sorry for him. But it's nothing to be ashamed of."

"No, of course it isn't. And it wasn't a major seizure. Jason has petit mal, nothing worse. But, boy, he avoided me like the plague after that. You see, to someone like Jason, who always took great pride in being suave as all get-out, it would be an intolerable affliction . . . to be so out of control and . . . helpless. No one at school knew about it—except Andre, of course. I think Jason lived in fear for a while there, thinking I might blab it around."

"Too bad he didn't know what I know," she said, giving him a soft kiss, "that you're a good man."

"You know, you're cute when you're biased," he said, rubbing the back of her neck. "Tell me, Miss O'Roarke, how soon do you figure we can blow this joint?"

Jocelyn, who was about to say "I'll get my coat," checked her response when she saw a figure enter from the far end of the living room. "Uh . . . not just yet, my dear. We are about to see King Kong meet Godzilla."

Conversations everywhere halted as Jason Saylin, with Courtney glued to his side, strode across the room, making a beeline for Irene and Marc. With slow deliberation Irene detached herself from Marc and solemnly turned to face her nemesis, waiting for him to make the first move. The whole room waited with her and all were rewarded; it was quite a move. Saylin beat three times on the left lapel of his Giorgio Armani suit and sank to one knee, saying, "Mea culpa, mea culpa. I kneel corrected. You *are* Hedda."

There was a huge burst of applause and cheers, and only Jocelyn noticed the fleeting look of profound relief which crossed Irene's face before she said, "I am amazed and know not what to say . . . except it's all fettucine over the dam, as far as I'm concerned!"

There was much hand shaking and backslapping amidst the laughter and popping of champagne corks. Jocelyn let out a long-held breath, hoping that the worst was over, but somehow she didn't think so. Try as she might to quell her skepticism, she still felt like she had just watched an installment of *Theatre on Walton's Mountain* with miscast players. The only other person who seemed to share her misgivings was Andre, who scurried about the room emptying ashtrays and rubbing his hands together, looking like the White Rabbit, only twice as anxious.

Her train of thought was broken by Phillip's elbow poking her rib cage. "Look alive, matey. We're about to face inspection."

A beaming Courtney bore down on them with Saylin in tow.

"Jason, honey, this is my dear friend, Joshie O'Roarke. And, I believe, you already know her fella."

"Indeed, I do. How are you, Phil? It's been too, too long. Must say, it's a surprise to find you mingling with us show folk. Knowing his preference for cold fact over fancy, I must credit you, Miss O'Roarke, as a veritable Circe for having lured him here," Saylin said, bending his thin angular body over Jocelyn's hand in the Continental manner. Jocelyn smiled and muttered something inane, suppressing an impulse to curtsey and an even stronger impulse to guffaw while thinking, Christ! The guy really talks like this. Where am I—Masterpiece Party?

Before Jocelyn's whimsey got the better of her, Courtney piped in, "I don't know about any Circe, sugar, but Joshie is a regular siren, that's for sure. Why, I remember, when we were in St. Louis, she had more boys around that backstage than you'd find flies around—"

Swiftly finding her tongue, Jocelyn broke in, "You have a lovely apartment, Jason. I'd love to see more of it. Someone told me you even have a greenhouse."

A look of genuine pleasure spread across Saylin's face. "Why, yes, I do. I've had the terrace glassed in and converted into one. It took a lot of time and money and everyone thought I was mad to do it. But it was well worth it. It's the only thing that keeps me sane during these dreadful New York winters. Would you like to see it?"

Phillip and Jocelyn nodded, and Saylin turned to Courtney,

whose bright smile almost, but not quite, concealed the look of "Here we go again" in her eyes. Jason, in his first flush of enthusiasm, failed to notice.

"Dear heart, could you go and fetch our guest of honor? I'm sure Irene and Marc would like to join our little tour. There's a love."

Five minutes later, Phillip, Jocelyn, Irene, Marc and Franklin Allen were being led by Jason and Courtney through Saylin's private tropical forest. The terrace cum greenhouse ran the length of the apartment and faced Central Park, making an impressive juxtaposition to the chilly winter scene below. As Saylin waxed poetic on the horticultural history of some of his favorite specimens, Jocelyn took care to avoid Phillip's gaze. Phillip knew that Jocelyn had an incurable chalk thumb and took about as much interest in gardening as W. C. Fields took in children. He was having a wonderful time watching her careful impersonation of a garden club lady.

"The poinsettias are Courtney's little traditional touch for the holidays. And that little magnolia tree over there in the corner, she dug up out of her grandmother's yard last time she was in Georgia . . . Adds a quaint touch, don't you think? These calla lilies are my particular pride and joy. I sent a cutting from one of them to Kate Hepburn on her last birthday and got a delightful note back. Can't wait to get her over here to see these beauties, though . . ."

Everyone made the appropriate oohing and aahing noises as they continued down the long room. Luckily, Irene had had the foresight to bring a bottle of Moët with her, which she and Jocelyn passed freely back and forth. Jocelyn had given up trying to commune with hothouse flora and was intently studying Saylin. With his long limbs, his thin, beaky nose and his wispy brown hair, he looked like a stork with a good tailor. Despite the flush brought to his cheeks, either by excitement or humidity, he was not a particularly attractive man. This made Jocelyn wonder a bit. She knew Courtney had as fond an eye as any woman for a handsome frame, her taste in the past had leaned toward dark-eyed Mediterranean types. But then again, Jason was not without a certain erudite charm, the kind that goes over well on talk shows and panel discussions, both of which had made Saylin the most visible theatre critic in New York, if not the best. That would matter to Courtney, just as it would matter to her mama and grandma. If a Southern lady is going to hook up with a "Yankee," he had better *be* somebody!

As Jason was drawing to the end of his dissertation, something caught Jocelyn's eye. A long, low table, covered with a well-ordered array of foliage, ran along the inside wall of the terrace, with various tools and containers of potting soil, plant food and the like stored underneath. But the tiny silver spoon perched on the table's edge wasn't, Jocelyn felt sure, used for leaf feeding, nor was there any possible botanical use for the small hand mirror, covered with traces of a white powder, which lay alongside it.

She was about to nudge Phillip when, looking up, she found Jason Saylin staring straight at her. The flush had left his face and, for a moment, his mouth worked soundlessly. Phillip's earlier hunch had been correct.

"Well . . . uh . . . time to rejoin the party, don't you think? No need to backtrack. We can go through here," he said, swiftly sliding open a glass door which led into the master bedroom. It was a good ploy as far as Jocelyn was concerned. If anything could distract her, looking at someone else's bedroom could. And it was quite a bedroom at that. The walls were covered in dove-gray watered silk and there was an opulent white satin comforter on the king-sized bed. The only thing missing was Jean Harlow. Next to a crystal vase holding two delicate stalks of rubrum lilies, she spied a bottle of Courtney's favorite scent, Red, and out of the corner of her eye she saw a fluffy pegnoir hanging in the bathroom.

There were two other doors, one which obviously led back out to the living room. Jocelyn asked about the other.

"Oh, that leads to my study," Saylin said, pleased to keep the conversation on safe ground. "Would you like to see it?"

"You mean, the lion's den," Jocelyn said. "How could I resist?"

The first thing they noticed as Jason swung open the door was not the massive oak desk or the English Squire decor, but the man behind the desk. Andre Guérisseur stood in front of an IBM Selectric with a piece of typing paper in his hand. He blushed deeply, like a small boy caught with his hand in the cookie jar, and quickly slid the paper into a desk drawer.

"Oh . . . ah, there you all are! Thought the Venus's-flytrap might've got you," he joked feebly. "Miss Ingersoll, I think some friends of yours have just arrived. They were asking for you."

"Ah! Tom Selleck, no doubt, come to beg for my favors," Irene pronounced grandly. "Well, Marc honey, it's been swell, but Tinsel Town calls."

Carson gave her a smart slap on the behind as she sailed past him, saying, "Cheeky bitch! Luckily, I am an understanding man and I know this is something you've waited a lifetime for, my darling . . . the chance to sell out!"

Coming from anyone besides Carson, such a gibe would have immediately elicted Irene's well-known glacier gaze, which could transmit frostbite at forty paces. Instead, she threw back her head and hooted, "You bet your sweet ass, lover! They can even put me in a sitcom and call it *Hedda, Dearest* . . . wouldn't that be a laugh, Jason?"

The flush was returning to Saylin's cheeks as Irene and Marc plunged back in to the living room. Jocelyn grabbed Phillip's hand and followed suit, leaving Jason, Andre and Franklin grouped around the desk. As soon as they negotiated their way back to the bar, Jocelyn lit a cigarette and asked, "Did you see what I saw out on the terrace?"

Phillip nodded. "Yup . . . and I saw Jason see Jocelyn see. Jocelyn sees coke. Look, Spot, look, see Jason turn white!"

"I'm so glad Sesame Street paid off for you," Jocelyn said dryly. "Irene noticed it, too, smarty."

"How do you know?"

"Because she was cocky enough to make that *Hedda, Dearest* crack . . . That's what she overheard Jason say in the Gardenia, right before the fettucine hit the fan. I knew their little kiss-and-make-up act was too good to last."

"Well, she's had a lot of champagne."

"Who hasn't?" Jocelyn asked, reaching for a fresh glass.

An hour later they still hadn't managed to make a graceful exit. It never failed to amaze Jocelyn that she always knew all the gossip about everybody—except herself. Since the Harriet Weldon case, it seemed that she and Phillip had been touted as the new Nick and

Nora Charles of the Great White Way. At one point someone even asked her if she had a terrier.

Andre had snatched Phillip from her side and was introducing him to all and sundry. Despite his apparent fatigue he was doing alright, judging from the excited laughter his every comment drew from the more available ladies in the room. To distract the little green-eyed monster gnawing at her insides, Jocelyn was intently watching the other people about her.

Jason Saylin had emerged from the study bright-eyed and bushy-tailed. At odd intervals he would collect a friend or two and return to the study. After a few minutes the friends would return to the party wearing the same eyes and tails. Better living through chemicals, Jocelyn thought. Saylin had obviously gotten over his fear of Phillip blowing the whistle and was having a few toots among friends. As the evening progressed, his circle of friends grew larger. At one point she even saw Marc and Franklin slipping off with him, with Marc merrily humming, "Let it snow, let it snow, let it snow" under his breath.

Courtney Mason, professional friend to the famous or about-to-be-famous, had Irene cornered in the dining alcove for what looked like a serious heart-to-heart talk. Remembering that Irene had once referred to Courtney as "Barbara Walters's Southern cousin," Jocelyn drifted toward the alcove with the shameless intention of eavesdropping. But all she caught was Courtney saying, "Irenie, honey, I just have to show you something" as Courtney rose and led Irene off toward the master bedroom. Before she could decide whether the "something" was a Halston original or a new vibrator, Jocelyn was accosted by a drunken playwright who belligerently demanded to know if she didn't think *Raging Bull* was the penultimate fight film. It was a debate that he had obviously begun elsewhere, but it struck a nerve and she spent a good twenty minutes carefully and eloquently explaining why she thought it was *not*. She was winding down with ". . . and just because he's one hell of an actor, don't expect me to get all warm and runny over a character who's essentially a crummy little pimp!" when Gerrard came up and patted her arm.

"Calm down, tiger," he said, turning to the nearly sobered playwright. "Give up, fella, you're dealing with a purist. She's seen Robert Ryan in *The Set Up* six times."

"Damn right," Jocelyn spluttered as the other man weaved away, "not to mention Garfield in *Body and Soul* and Jimmy Cagney in—"

"Jocelyn, Josh, my love, my own . . . it's time to go home."

"Hey, that rhymed," she chuckled. Then, looking in his face, she repented. "God, you must be beat . . . and you've got a report to file in the morning! Oh, love, I'm sorry to keep you out so late."

"For a self-professed agnostic, your Catholic guilt reflex is still pretty sharp," he said fondly. "You didn't break my arm to keep me here and I'm glad I came. I learned a few things."

"Like what?"

"Like your peers have a very high opinion of your talent and think you should become a very big director lady. Why don't you go for it?"

Jocelyn shrugged. It was too late in the day or early in the morning to pursue this particular topic.

"I don't know . . . it's hard . . . it's a man's market . . . and I'm scared witless! And right now I just want to get you home to bed. Tomorrow I'm gonna make a great omelette and send you off ready to face the world . . . and Tommy Zito."

Like most of Jocelyn's domestic resolutions, this one was doomed to come to naught, but this time for the worst of reasons. Just as they were about to go for their coats, the door of the study burst open and Jason Saylin came staggering into the room, looking like a puppet who'd just been electrocuted. His limbs jerked spasmodically and his eyes rolled back in his head. A crazed pirouette landed him on his back in the middle of the living room where he continued to jerk and writhe.

Phillip raced toward him, pulling a steel pen out his pocket and calling over his shoulder to Jocelyn, "Call 911! Try to find his medication!"

The next few minutes were like living inside a kaleidoscope, with fragmented impressions all around—Phillip kneeling on top of Jason with Andre close behind him, the pandemonium in the room drowned out by Courtney's high, shrill scream, "*No! No! No!* He can't—"

As she dashed toward the phone, Jocelyn stopped to grab Courtney by the shoulders and administer a sharp slap.

"If you want to help him, go find his medication! I'll call the ambulance."

Her words had the desired effect. As she stood by the oak desk in the study, glancing down at an overturned vial of white powder, she heard Courtney madly scrambling through the medicine cabinet in the adjoining room.

The ambulance made it in good time—but not quite good enough. By the time the two white-coated medics entered the penthouse, Saylin's seizure had subsided, along with his breathing and all other vital signs.

No one there was qualified to make the statement, but as they watched the stretcher roll out of the apartment, followed by Courtney with Andre trailing behind, there wasn't one amongst them who didn't know, with an awful certainty, that Jason Saylin was dead.

CHAPTER V

"Hello, this is Jocelyn. I'm not home right now but if you leave your name and number . . ."

Fitting her key in the lock, Jocelyn heard the familiar drone of her voice on the answering machine. She was totally bushed from teaching a five-hour acting class, but it had provided a welcome distraction after the horrors of the previous evening. However, wanting nothing but a hot bath and a tall drink, she wearily tugged off her down coat without the slightest intention of picking up the receiver. Let the machine earn its keep, she thought and was halfway to the bathroom when the voice on the line stopped her.

"Hello, Jocelyn, this is Andre Guérisseur. Could you please call me as soon as you get in at Jas———, at the penthouse? The number is 87—"

Before he reached the third digit, she was on the phone.

"Andre, yes, I'm here. Just got home. Hold on a second while I shut this damn thing off. There, that does it . . . Andre, I'm so terribly sorry about Jason. Phillip called this morning and told me. Are you alright?"

"Oh, I'm holding up, I g-guess. There's been a lot to deal with . . . the press and all and making arrangements for the . . . uh . . . services." He paused for a moment as if winded. "Jason had hardly any f-family to speak of, so I've sort of assumed that role. I thought Courtney might but . . . well . . ."

There was another pause; this one went on longer until Jocelyn gently prodded, "You thought Courtney might want to handle . . . things?"

"Yes, I did," he said, adding quickly, "and that's why I called—I mean, not about the funeral, about C-Courtney. I'm rather worried about her, you see."

"Well, Andre, I'm sure she's in shock."

"Yes, yes, of course, you're right . . . but, all the same, I'm very concerned. This morning at the hospital when we were officially notified that Jason was . . . d-dead, we took a cab back to the penthouse. She never said a word, all the way back. And, as soon as we got here, she packed a bag and went back to her old apartment on the East Side. It was all I could do to get her to tell me where she was g-going. I've phoned several times but her roommate just says that she can't come to the phone."

Hearing the note of anguish in his voice, she felt sympathy mixed with irritation. Men can be so dense, she thought, but what she said was, "Andre, she's just not up to talking to anyone right now. As for leaving the apartment, you have to understand that, for a high-strung girl like Courtney, it would be more than she could take to stay on in the place where she saw her lover die—especially with the police running in and out all day."

"Yes, that's true," he said, sounding only half-convinced, "and thank God for Phillip. He's been a real b-brick. It's just that I thought I'd be the one person she'd turn to now . . . Oh, I know that sounds presumptuous, but we were very close—she and Jason and I, really like family. I'd just like to know how she is and I thought . . . I thought maybe you c-could speak with her and let me know."

"Me?! I . . . Andre, I'd like to help but Courtney and I aren't all that close, you know."

"Oh, I know," he said, too distressed to be tactful. "Courtney doesn't have very many women friends. But I think she'd talk to you. She thinks you're very . . . strong. And she needs someone's strength right now. P-Please call her, Jocelyn."

"Okay, Andre," she sighed. No stranger to the art of playing on others' heart strings, she realized that she had just been fiddled by a pro, but she managed to insert a minor stipulation. "Not tonight though. Let's give her a day's rest. I'll try to get ahold of her in the morning."

A bath and a hot meal of stir-fried chicken with peanuts lifted her spirits, but only minimally. When eleven o'clock rolled around and there was no word from Phillip Gerrard, she tossed aside her Robertson Davies novel, poured a glass of Chenin Blanc and turned on the late-night news to get the media version of Jason Saylin's demise. To her surprise, it went like this—"Noted theatre critic Jason Saylin died at his home last night on New York's Upper West Side while hosting a party in honor of the Broadway opening of *Hedda Gabler*, starring Irene Ingersoll. A feature writer for *Metropolitan Magazine* and several other publications, Mr. Saylin was also a well-known lecturer and frequent guest on many talk shows. He was forty-one years old. The cause of death is still undetermined."

Undetermined?! What the hell? They must've done the autopsy by now! What are they dickering about?

In answer to her thoughts the intercom buzzed; it was Phillip. Seconds later she opened the door to a very tired and unhappy policeman. Adept at reading his moods, she seated him on the sofa and poured him a large Martell before launching her questions. Once he had settled in, she sat down beside him and said, "I just saw the news. Why the mystery about the cause of death? It can't matter to Jason now if the world knows he was epileptic."

"No, that doesn't matter . . . and it doesn't count," Phillip said, reaching for one of Jocelyn's cigarettes. It was a bad sign; Phillip was a reformed two-pack-a-day smoker and he only reverted when under duress. "Jason's seizure wasn't caused by his epilepsy. It wasn't that kind of seizure."

"But—then what? I know he was tooting like a train all evening but cocaine doesn't—"

"No, cocaine doesn't—but strychnine does. Jason had petit mal, not grand mal. That vial you saw in the study wasn't pure cocaine. The top layer of powder was strychnine. Inhaling pure strychnine induces a powerful seizure just before death. Jason Saylin was murdered. Murdered right under my nose," he said, viciously grinding out the half-smoked cigarette.

He took another sip of brandy and stared grimly into space. Logically they both knew that nothing short of dumb luck or genuine clairvoyance could have averted the killing, but Phillip was in the grips of what could only be described as professional pique. Jocelyn, no stranger to that mood, knew better than to offer consoling phrases. Instead she did the only helpful thing she could think of; she lit a log in the fireplace. If he's going to sit and stare for the next two hours, he might as well have something to stare at, she thought, feeling overwhelmed by the sense of helplessness and inadequacy she experienced whenever she ran smack into the harsh realities of Phillip's job.

Phillip studied the straight line of her back as Jocelyn crouched in front of the fireplace, one hand holding a lit taper and the other stroking her huge cat, Angus. He suddenly felt much better. She often had this affect on him. Sitting in a cold squad car on a long stakeout, he would think of her arguing passionately about a film or exhorting one of her students to "stop making the *safe* choices," and his weary vigil would become more bearable. Every day he dealt with the grim facts of death, but Jocelyn, in everything she did, was firmly committed to the stuff of life. In some inexplicable way, her commitment strengthened his.

It crossed his mind, and not for the first time, that he wanted to marry Jocelyn O'Roarke and should say so. Being a man who normally had no trouble coming to the point, especially when the point was something he wanted, it irked him to run up against his own timidity. What if she said no? And knowing that her old-fashioned respect for the institution of marriage went hand in hand with her enormous fear of it made the topic no easier to broach.

Still, as he watched the firelight play across her face and pick up the red highlights in her hair, he knew he was ready to cross some kind of Rubicon. Softly he said, "Josh."

She turned toward him, raising a quizzical eyebrow and cocking her head toward the fire. "Better?"

"Umm, much . . . better still if you'd trot yourself back over here."

"We aim to please," she said, curling up next to him on the sofa and settling in. "So, let me ask you this—"

"No, wait. There's something I'd like to ask you first."

"Oh, listen, if it's about Irene, don't worry. She's my friend and all but you've got your job to do and she has to be questioned like everyone else, I know. Still she has no possible motive now that—"

"No, no," he said urgently, not wanting the moment to slip away, "not about that . . . something else. See, I have this idea that we—"

It was an idea whose time had not yet come. The phone began to ring, and the voice on the answering machine was that of Andre Guérisseur's, trying to locate Phillip. He took the call in the bedroom and when he emerged, five minutes later, the suitor had been replaced by the detective. One look at his face prompted Jocelyn to throw another log on the fire.

"What did Andre have to say?"

"He saw the late-night news. Andre's pretty quick at putting two and two together. He figured that if there's something fishy about Jason's death he should let me know."

"Know what?" she asked, crossing to the bar to pour herself a drink. Something in Phillip's tone told her that she'd need one.

"Well," he sighed, "Andre didn't notice until he got back from the hospital this afternoon, but something's missing from the apartment—the review of *Hedda*. Saylin drafted the notice right after the show, before his guests arrived. That's what Andre was slipping in the drawer when we came in to the study."

Trying to ignore the goosebumps that were crawling up her arms, she said, "Well, that's odd, certainly. But not highly ominous."

"Josh, Andre read the review . . . It was a pan."

CHAPTER VI

The next morning found Jocelyn practicing her private ritual of Better Homes Through Avoidance, wherein all her wayward and latent bent for housekeeping blossomed into full force in order to shield her from an even more dismal task. It worked like this. On her way to the phone to call Courtney, she noticed the rug needed vacuuming. Three hours later the furniture was waxed, the floors were mopped and the long-suffering stove had been degreased. A faint mist of room deodorizer hung in the air while Angus crouched in the bedroom loft shooting Jocelyn loathsome glances. The phone was still untouched and undusted . . . and there was nothing left to clean.

With a philosophical shrug she picked up the receiver and started dialing Courtney's number, feeling that after you've just scoured your toilet bowl for the first time since your last big party, how much worse could things get?

When the phone was picked up before the second ring Jocelyn instantly knew that she'd be talking not to Courtney but to her sometimes roommate, Patsy Snell. Patsy was a fortyish lighting designer who had done a lot of operas and worked with enough real divas to be able to take Courtney in her stride.

"Hi, Patsy . . . It's Jocelyn O'Roarke. How are you?"

"Could be better," Patsy barked back in her typical clipped style. "Listen—wanted to tell you—met a fine young actor in my last show, name's Jon. Does Shakespeare like a hungry Olivier . . . just great. Scared to death of contemporary comedy, though. I gave him your number. Told him if anybody could make him feel comfortable with shtick, you could. Hope he calls."

"Well, gee . . . thanks a heap," Jocelyn said with a wince. Patsy was an old master of the left-handed compliment sprinkled with grains of truth. But she was the best kind of theatre woman in that she liked talent for talent's sake and liked to see good people get work and get better.

"Listen, Patsy, the reason I called . . . I just wanted to know how Courtney was doing?"

"Hard to say. She can't seem to decide if she's Jackie Kennedy or Ophelia. Won't come to the phone either."

"Oh, well, in that case," Jocelyn said, trying to suppress great waves of relief.

"Wait . . . hold on a second, Josh. She just got up."

There was a scrambling sound at the other end, and then Courtney Mason's voice came through, soft and laconic. "Joshie . . . that you, darlin'?"

"Yes. Courtney, I . . . uh . . . just wanted to know if you were alright and if there was anything I can do?"

"That's too dear, just too dear," Courtney paused with a catch in her voice. "I haven't really been able to . . . take things in yet. It all seems too crazy and I just . . . don't know. But I know there's things I should be doin', gettin' in order. I just can't seem to . . ."

"Well, if you need any help . . ."

"You know, Joshie, I guess I do. I need some help . . . or something. Could you maybe stop by today?"

"Why . . . sure. I'd be glad to. I'll see you this afternoon."

Jocelyn hung up, walked briskly in to her bathroom, kicked the toilet and said, "There's a sucker born every minute."

Ninety minutes later she was in the brusque but vise-like embrace of Patsy Snell, standing in the hallway of her East Seventy-sixth Street apartment. Patsy, in gray wool slacks and a Calvin Klein shirt, swiftly broke the clinch and stood back to critically assess Jocelyn. "You look good, kid. Could play ingenue a few more years with enough bastard amber gels."

"Patsy, you're too kind. Now, before I slit my wrists, where's Courtney?"

"Where else? In the bedroom and in the dumps. You got your work cut out for you, kiddo. The doctor's got her half-loopy on tranquilizers, but it's not helping much. I think withdrawal's about to set in."

"Withdrawal? What do you mean?"

"Oh, come on, cookie! You know the score. Courtney was always a nice Southern girl who sipped Chablis and took a polite puff on a joint when it was offered. But she's been keeping company with Snortin' Saylin for the last two years. Every day was Christmas and now that there's no light powder on the ground, it's beginning to make her a little jumpy."

"Oh . . . I didn't know that Courtney did that much coke."

"Hey, honey, in that club if you didn't toot, you didn't get to play with the band . . . know what I mean?"

"Makes sense. Listen, Patsy, has Courtney seen or heard any of the latest news reports?"

"You mean, does she know that her boyfriend was bumped off? Least that's how I figure it. No, she doesn't and I'm not about to tell her. The police will soon enough and it's tax money well spent as far as I'm concerned."

Without further ado Patsy trotted off toward Courtney's bedroom with a befuddled Jocelyn following in her wake. It was a small bedroom of uninteresting proportions but decorated with taste. The dominant pieces were a queen-sized bed, with a patchwork quilt, and a rattan headboard, and an antique dressing table with an enormous mirror.

The faint light of a winter afternoon seeped through the half-open venetian blinds, revealing to Jocelyn something new and different—Courtney Mason looking dreadful. The style was still there, enhanced by a delicately tinted Mary McFadden lounging robe, but the content was a mess. Courtney's abundant red hair was uncombed and matted, her skin looked as if she'd mistaken her ashtray for a powder box and her eyes, large to begin with, were what Keene paintings came from.

Seemingly unaware of the presence of the other two women, she stood by the window with a large tumbler of Chablis on the sill and stared down at the traffic on Second Avenue, muttering, "So many little cars. Where do they all think they're goin'?"

Turning to leave, Patsy nudged Jocelyn and whispered, "At least they're not *streetcars*. Good luck . . . Stella."

As she took a tentative step toward Courtney, Jocelyn felt as if she were having one of her bad "actor dreams," the kind where you find yourself onstage suddenly in a play you don't recognize, wearing nothing but a slip and not knowing what your next line is or what part you're playing. Given Courtney's stance of queenly tragedy, Jocelyn figured her own role was lady-in-waiting and her next line would be, "What ails my fair sovereign?" which she freely paraphrased into "Courtney, how're you feeling?"

"Dead . . . just dead, Joshie. I feel cold all the time. No matter what I do, I just think of Jason lying in a box somewhere . . . and I get cold. It's like everything . . . stopped."

"Well, it's a horrible shock. I won't say anything stupid like, 'I know what you're going through'—because I don't, not firsthand, anyway. But I can imagine how you—"

"We were going to be married in the spring, did you know that?" Courtney asked dreamily, as a long-fingered hand picked up the glass of wine and drained half of it. "I didn't want a winter wedding . . . too dreary. I had the bridesmaids' dresses all picked out. You want to see the designs?"

Too shocked to do anything but nod dumbly, she watched as Courtney, with sudden animation, pulled out a stack of *Bride* magazines. The next half hour was spent sitting on the bed as Courtney pored through back issues, earnestly discussing the pros and cons of pastel colors. They had worked their way through the entire spectrum, with no end to the macabre fashion show in sight, when Courtney flipped to a page that had a full-color photo of a tall, distinguished-looking bridegroom in a dove gray tuxedo. Looking at the inverted photo Jocelyn could see that the model bore a faint resemblance to Jason. Courtney shivered slightly and slugged down the rest of the wine. Holding the glass out with an unsteady hand, she asked, "Joshie, could you be an angel and get me a little more Chablis? I'm feelin' all icy again. The bar's in the living room . . . Oh, get yourself something, too. I apologize for bein' such a sorry hostess."

Touched by this feeble attempt at nice manners, Jocelyn grabbed the glass and beat a hasty retreat to the living room. Patsy Snell sat hunched over an ancient drafting board, working on an elaborate lighting plot. As Jocelyn shakily poured herself a diet soda and made Courtney a wine cooler with lots of ice and soda, Patsy shot her a wry look and asked, "How's it going in there?"

"Whew! Not too good. It seems she's well past her Jackie O and

Ophelia stages and has just entered her full-fledged Blanche Dubois period. I guess you saw that coming, huh?"

"Yeah . . . it's the logical progression after all. I'm big on logic —which makes me wonder"—Patsy paused to study Jocelyn's face for a brief but intense moment—"makes me wonder exactly why the hell you called today? Now don't go all huffy on me, O'Roarke. I know you're a sweetheart. One of the last of the rough-tough cream puffs rumor has it. But you and Courtney have never been all that tight. Matter of fact, ol' Courtney doesn't really like you all that much."

"Then why in blazes did you let her drag me over here?!"

" 'Cause she respects you . . . and she's a little afraid of you. Has been ever since you raked her ass over the coals in Philly when she was walking through that play you did together. Thought you might have the old cold-shower effect on her . . . But I'd still like to know why you *came.* Your boyfriend ask you to?"

"Hell no, Patsy! Phillip doesn't work like that. It's nothing like that," Jocelyn protested, but Patsy's bird-like gaze continued to bore into her. "Well, it's *something* like that. Andre Guérisseur called last night and asked me to get in touch with Courtney. He's not sure what to do about funeral arrangements and wanted to consult Courtney. Also, he's worried about her."

"Like *hell* he is!" Courtney's booming voice reverberated around the room, making the other two women jump. All traces of the languishing waif vanished as she prowled the room like a nervous cat, hair flying, eyes bright and feverish. "He doesn't give a good goddamn about me, the bug-eyed little toad. It's all for show—all for show. Hateful little hypocrite! He'd just as soon see Jason buried in a pinewood box in a pauper's cemetery for all he cares!"

"Easy, Courtney," Jocelyn said, looking to Patsy for help. But Patsy had wisely decided to withdraw from the field and was, once again, bent over her drafting board, leaving Jocelyn to play Mary Worth. "Look, you may not like Andre but he was Jason's oldest friend."

"Friend?! He was no friend—just a leech, a blood-sucking little leech. And Jason was so good to him, so loyal. But he used Jason, used his contacts and his influence . . . and just left him flat."

"Left him?"

"Yes, he was just about to," Courtney said, nodding her head adamantly. "He got himself some fancy teaching job in a stuffy old college somewhere. He was just staying on until . . . the wedding. Poor Jason was so confused and hurt, didn't know where to turn because he'd gotten so awfully . . . dependent on Andre. I told him not to worry, that I'd take care of things for him. But he still fretted about it, offered Andre a raise, a new car, a trip to Europe—anything he wanted. But that little Judas just said it was time for him to do his own work and that was that! Conceited worm . . . If anything killed Jason that . . ."

Courtney's voice trailed off as she narrowed her eyes and scrutinized the two other women as if she were seeing them for the first time. Rejuvenated by her wrath, things were now beginning to filter through.

"What was that Patsy said about your boyfriend? He's a policeman . . . Why should he want you to see me?"

"Courtney, I can't really say. It's not my place and no one's really sure yet—"

The distraught woman crossed directly to Jocelyn and grabbed her roughly by the shoulders. "You know something! Somebody's told you something and I want to know what it *is!*"

"No. Nobody's told me anything," Jocelyn said, breaking free from Courtney's hold. She wasn't about to divulge what Phillip had told her privately, but there was no longer any point in trying to spare Courtney. "It's just that the coroner hasn't announced the cause of death yet. So you have to prepare yourself for the possibility that Jason may not have died from natural causes."

"He was killed . . . You're sayin' he was *killed!*"

She buried her face in her hands and stood in the center of the room, swaying dangerously. Patsy and Jocelyn moved toward her simultaneously. Just before they reached her, she raised pleading eyes to them and wailed, "My God, you see what he's done? You see what that man has done?!"

Jocelyn stopped dead in her tracks, but Patsy caught Courtney just before she hit the floor.

CHAPTER VII

While Jocelyn was looking at bridesmaids' dresses with Courtney, Phillip Gerrard was driving over to Manhattan Plaza with a disgruntled Tommy Zito in tow to see Irene Ingersoll. Tommy was having a lousy day. It began with his wife, Marion—a great cook but a hopeless housekeeper—scorching his favorite shirt, and it had gone downhill from there. Normally the most impartial of policemen, he was very partial, indeed, toward Irene Ingersoll and it bothered him. It wasn't, he told himself, more or less truthfully, a matter of having the hots for her; it was more a matter of . . . respect. But respect was too mild a term for what Zito felt about the statuesque actress who had given him his first glimpse of what great acting was all about; reverence was more like it. In his present state of mind, the idea of questioning Irene about a murder was as distasteful as booking a nun for shoplifting.

"Aw, Phil, gimme a break," he said, rubbing his face with both hands. "What could she have to do with Saylin getting bumped off? Even if she saw his crummy review, it ain't likely she happened to have a packet of strychnine handy in her evening bag to lace his coke with, is it?"

"Of course not," Gerrard snapped back. "I don't think anybody *brought* the stuff, Tommy! It seems too farfetched . . . at this stage anyway. Right now, it strikes me as a spur-of-the-moment crime. But that's just a hunch based on my tour of Jason's little greenhouse. He had enough weed killer on that terrace to choke a jungle. I don't know enough about gardening to guess what's in that stuff but, if somebody did, they might know what to grab in a hurry. Anyhow, the lab boys should have the word on that by tonight."

"Oh . . . so that's why you had the pathologist check for it!

That was pretty sharp, Phil. A regular autopsy wouldn't have picked that up."

"No, that wasn't the main reason. Remember I saw Jason have a seizure once before. It wasn't anywhere near as violent as this one. That's what made me think. I read a textbook case once of a young child who'd got hold of his mother's strychnine and inhaled it. She used it as an aphrodisiac. The seizure described in the book was like Jason's, it seemed."

Tommy shook his head in dumb admiration. He was a good cop, but Phillip Gerrard was a smart one, the smartest he'd ever come across. You could trust Phil to know what he was doing, and if anybody could handle this interview with Miss Ingersoll, he could, Zito felt sure.

Phillip, for his part, felt nothing of the sort—far from it. This was the first case he'd ever worked on where he'd known the people involved, and it troubled him deeply. Try as he would, there was no disguising the fact that, as things stood now, Irene Ingersoll was his chief suspect. It all came down to motive and she had it in spades. Side issues, like Jocelyn's affection for the woman, could not be considered nor allowed to sway him, and they wouldn't. But he dreaded the repercussions and sensed, with a fatalistic certainty, that this case would either make or break their relationship.

They parked the car on Tenth Avenue and took the elevator up to the fifteenth floor. Marc Carson greeted them at the door in jeans and a sweatshirt and ushered them into the bright but incredibly messy living room. The remnants of a late breakfast mingled on the coffee table with piles of books and scripts. Every ashtray was filled to overflowing and an empty vodka bottle stood on the floor by the futon sofa.

Although it was past noon, Carson was rubbing sleep out of his eyes.

"Sorry, fellas. You'll have to forgive us. It was a late night. Irenie will be out in a minute. Can I get you some coffee?"

Gerrard and Zito politely refused the offer despite the fact that they were both five-cups-a-day men. It was a small attempt to maintain a professional distance in this chaotically homey and informal environment. Irene's entrance, in an Indian-print caftan with her long blond hair spilling around her shoulders, did nothing to enhance the seriousness of the situation. Zito thought that she looked tired, disheveled and absolutely glorious.

"Phillip . . . Thomas, how are you, dears? Or shouldn't I ask? After all, this isn't a social call, so personal questions might be a little outré. Just let me get some caffeine into my system before we get down to business. Okay?"

The two detectives waited uncomfortably as Carson fixed a mug of coffee with a small dollop of brandy and brought it to Irene. As Marc settled himself on the arm of the sofa, she took a long sip, patted his hand and placed the cup on the cluttered coffee table.

"Alright, let 'er rip. I know you've got a job to do. But, please, no 'Miss Ingersoll' stuff. We all had a few drinks together the other night, so let's keep it on a first-name basis, okay?"

Her effortless aplomb left Tommy Zito breathless, but Phillip swiftly took the bull by the horns. "That's fine, Irene. Let me tell you why we're here. Jason Saylin didn't die from an epileptic seizure. He died from inhaling strychnine that was laced in his cocaine. We have no reason to think that his death was a suicide, so that leaves us with only one other possible conclusion, you see. Now . . . let me say right off, we have no interest in the drug aspect of his death. A lot of people were doing coke that night. That's their business. I'm only interested in the actual cause of his death and, for that reason, I need to know the specific movements of the people who were present. That includes you and Marc. Now, right up until the time of Jason's tour of his greenhouse, you both were in plain view. I need to know where you both were after that and anything you saw or did. Irene, why don't you start."

She lit a Camel and reached for her coffee, then looked up at Gerrard with a rueful smile. "You're asking a lot from a woman who consumed more than her fair share of champagne last night . . . but I'll try. As you know, I left the study when Andre came in to say some friends of mine had arrived—some old pals from Equity Library Theatre. So Marc and I went out to greet them. We all toasted each other with more bubbly and started reminiscing about this god-awful production of *Miss Julie* that we'd done together years ago—at the time, we'd dubbed it *Miss Ghouly.* Anyway, one old story led to another and pretty soon Marc got bored and . . . wandered off." She paused to shoot a brief, questioning glance at

Carson. "Then . . . let me see . . . oh, yes, Maxine Knox—she's an agent—came up and dragged me off to meet her newest protégé. Some pimply kid who's writing the definitive play about herpes. He started telling me *all* about it. You can imagine how enthralled I was. About the time he got around to asking me if I'd consider playing Bacteria, I decided I needed another drink and made a mad dash for the bar. Unfortunately, when I got there Courtney got hold of me . . . Now that was bizarre. I mean, Courtney's what we call a 'Fame Fan'—if you're hot then you're one of her *dearest* friends. But, with me, she'd obviously decided we were more than friends—we were *sisters!* She got me sequestered in that dining alcove and started pouring it on in a big way. A lot of it was just rambling. I assumed that was the coke. Her basic point seemed to be that we were real soul mates because we both had achieved artistry without relinquishing our 'femininity.' Could you *gag?!* I mean, really, it was just a way to get a cheap shot in at Jo——" Irene stopped short and shook her head sharply as a faint flush came to her cheeks. "Lord, I'm just blathering. This can't possibly help . . ."

"No, please, go on with what you were saying." Gerrard's voice was perfectly calm, but Tommy spotted a telltale line of tension in his jaw. "No detail is too small not to have a possible bearing on the case. Go on."

"Aw, hell," Irene sighed and lit another Camel. "She made this tacky crack about 'poor Joshie, who's so brilliant but so brittle.' I wanted to deck her, I really did! But she was the hostess and a cat fight was definitely *not* in order. So I just ignored it and she took the hint. After that she changed the subject and started raving about her wedding plans. Made me nervous as hell. I thought any second she was going to ask me to be a bridesmaid—and I *hate* chiffon. Then she invited me into the bedroom to look at swatches . . . fabric swatches! Christ, the things we do to get a decent review!"

"And did you?"

"Huh? Did I what?"

"Get a decent review?"

"Yeah, most of them have been terrific . . . If you mean

Jason's, it never came out. I assume he hadn't written it before he . . . died."

"But he did, Irene," Phillip said with quiet insistence. "He wrote it before his guests arrived. It wasn't printed because it disappeared, along with the carbon. But Andre Guérisseur saw it. He was slipping it into the drawer as we came into the study. He wanted it put out of sight because it was far from favorable. Didn't you know that? Didn't you take a peek in that drawer on your way back from the bedroom?"

Irene shook her head slowly, as if it had suddenly become very heavy, and rose to her feet, clutching the folds of her gown. "No, that's not . . . that *can't* be true. Franklin said it would be . . ."

"Franklin said *what?* Said it would be in the bag if you agreed not to spill the story about Jason's cocaine habit to the press? That was the bargain, right? And you got double-crossed."

"Oh, my God," she gasped, staggering toward Gerrard. "She *told* you. You were there when I called Josh and she told you . . . How could she?! I trusted her . . . but I never meant, I never meant to . . ."

Marc Carson reached her before she reached Gerrard and spun her around by the shoulders. "Stop it, Irene! Just shut up," he said, shaking her.

Her five-foot ten-inch frame seemed to deflate as he deposited her back on the sofa. What his previous reticence had cost him became swiftly apparent as he turned a waxen face toward the other two men. "It wasn't her—it was me," he paused, panting like a marathon runner. "I was in the study . . . a couple of times. I . . . uh . . . did a few lines with Jason. The second time, Jason went out before me and I looked in that top drawer. I was curious. I read the review and it was lousy. Worse than the first one. I . . . couldn't see straight, I was so mad. Then I just crumpled the damn thing up and torched it in the ashtray."

"Both copies?"

"Both? I don't know. Wait a minute," he said, knitting his brows in a concentrated effort. "I can't say, really. When I opened the drawer, the review was right there. I didn't even take it out to read it, in case somebody came in the room. Then, when I did, I just reached in and mashed it up in my fist. I don't know if I picked up one sheet of paper or two. I just don't. Anyway, what difference does it make? It was a purely symbolic gesture on my part. I knew Jason would rewrite the damn piece in the morning but I wanted some time."

"Time for what?"

"Time to . . . break the news to Irenie," Carson said, kneading his knuckles.

It was only a brief hesitation, but Phillip sensed the other man's momentary confusion and pressed him. "But you didn't break the news, Marc, did you? Unless Irene's an even better actress than I think she is, she didn't know about that review until just now. So what kind of time were you stalling for? Time to figure out how to get Saylin? Or time to talk to someone who might be able to explain things—someone like Franklin Allen, maybe?"

There was a moment of perfect silence, but it was readily apparent to Gerrard and Zito that an intense conversation was taking place via the locked gazes of Marc and Irene. They were a couple, a close unit, coming to a major decision without the assistance of words. When Irene made the minutest of nods and lowered her eyes, Carson turned back to them with the air of a man about to face a firing squad.

"Alright, you win. It *was* Franklin. That's why Irene agreed to that whole nonsense about Jason's party and the reconciliation scene. Franklin said that in order to swing the move to Broadway, we had to pacify some backers. He didn't name names or explain why. But he also said it would insure a good review from Saylin. Again, no explanations other than pointing out that tipping the press to Jason's drug habit might hurt him a little but totally destroy our hopes for *Hedda.* So we agreed to bury the hatchet because he's . . . he was an influential critic and because we believed in this show. And you have no idea—trust me, none—how hard it is in these days of Reaganomics to mount a successful show on Broadway. We wanted *Hedda* to run with all our heart . . . But we wouldn't kill for it. That's a big difference."

By the end of this speech Carson had totally run out of steam, but Irene had managed to gain a second wind. "That's right, Phil. Compromise and homicide are a long way apart, you know. And you were right, I *didn't* know about that review. You can ask Court-ney. Marc was coming out of the study as she and I were heading into the master bedroom. So the review had already been burned. Besides, even if I saw the notice before Marc got to it—which I didn't—believe you me, you would've heard about it right away! When I think—" She stopped abruptly and turned toward Carson. "What the devil did it say, Marc?"

Phillip had a dangerous impulse to laugh as he watched Zito's eyes bulge and his jaw go slack. Tommy had a lot of experience despite his relative youth; he'd handled all sorts of suspects, hard-ened criminals and certifiable loonies alike, and very little fazed him. But with actors and their arcane sense of proportion he was as lost as Dorothy on her first day in Oz.

"Irene, now is *not* the time," Carson said, shaking his head wea-rily and showing a finer sense of priorities. "The point is—Irene was nowhere near that little vial of Jason's all evening. She never went into the study with him because she doesn't like cocaine—"

"Nope. Never saw what all the fuss was about it," she inter-jected. "I tried it once—gave me a nosebleed."

Carson overrode her and continued on a triumphant note. "Ac-tually, I don't see how *anybody* could've got at it. Jason kept it on him all night. He had it in this fancy little cut-glass container with a silver top. He said it was a Christmas gift from Courtney. So, every time we'd finish doing a line, he'd screw the top back on and put it in his breast pocket. Ask Franklin or any of the others—he never left the study without it. And there's another thing that's been giving me the willies ever since—have you considered the randomness of his death? I mean, if the strychnine was laced in that vial, any one of a half dozen of us might have taken that fatal hit rather than Jason. It's a miracle that he was the only one poisoned!"

"No, not really," Gerrard said quietly. "That possibility did oc-cur to us, of course, but only briefly. Jocelyn spotted it right away. When she was in the study phoning the ambulance, the vial was overturned on top of the desk. Even with the spillage it was still more than half-full. The way Saylin was doling it out that night, it should've been nearly empty. You see, the container on the desk, although it's identical to the one you described, was half-filled with poison. We found its twin—empty—in Saylin's dresser drawer. Somebody—the killer, that is—got at Jason's *private* stash."

CHAPTER VIII

"So, what's it gonna be, Josh? The booties or the bunting?"

"Aw, baby booties are boring. Besides, she'll get a ton of them from all her aunts who knit."

"So buy the bunting."

"I don't know. Do people really use buntings anymore?"

"Who knows? Who cares? At least people don't knit them! What's your problem today?!"

Jocelyn was wrangling with her best friend, Ruth Bernstein, in the infant's department of Saks. After her ordeal with Courtney and not wanting to go home and call Andre Guérisseur before she had a chance to talk with Phillip, she had called Ruth and asked her to help pick out a shower gift for their mutual friend Merle, who was due in May. In times of stress she fell back on the old motto— When the going gets tough, the tough go shopping. But today this strategy wasn't working as well as it usually did.

Normally an incisive shopper, she spent ten more minutes wallowing in indecision before settling on terry-cloth pajamas with bunny feet. Ruth, for whom patience was a learned skill, grabbed the package and marched away from the counter, muttering under her breath, "Boy, are you lucky. You don't toy with Saks's salesladies like that unless you want to risk life-long exile to Lamston's."

"Oh, lay off, Ruthie. It's been a rough day."

"Yeah, but you're an aunt six times over. I've seen you make faster purchases with your eyes closed. What is it . . . This Saylin thing?"

"Bingo." You could always count on Ruth to cut to the heart of the matter, even with a blunt scalpel.

"You saw Courtney today, huh? What gives with her?"

"Well . . . she's pretty wracked up, that's all," Jocelyn said, trying to hide her evasiveness. Her relationship with Ruth had always been predicated on total candor, but her relationship with Phillip demanded certain loyalties in terms of discretion and restraint. With anyone else it would have been easy; with Ruth it felt like the War Between the States.

They took the express elevator down to the main floor in constrained silence. Then Ruth did a sneaky thing. She ever so subtly angled Jocelyn over to the Pulse Points perfume counter. Like Galahad and the Holy Grail, Jocelyn had spent much of her life in quest of the perfect scent. Perfumes were a serious business with her, and as she approached the tray of testers on the counter with a certain grave formality, Ruth had a sudden inkling of what Madame Curie must have looked like toiling in her lab.

While Jocelyn was making an intense olfactory comparison between Bal à Versailles, and Fracas, Ruth asked with deceptive blandness, "You really love Phillip, Josh?"

She knocked over two bottles before replying, "Yeah, I guess I do . . . Why do you ask?"

"Well, I always knew you liked him a lot but lately you've been very mum about things. With you, that's a dead giveaway. The more you feel, the less you say. And right now you seem to be struggling with some huge conflict of interests, all of which leads me to believe two things. A—you're in love with a cop, and B—Saylin's death wasn't an accident."

Jocelyn placed the last tester on the counter with a smart click and turned to her old friend, her expression an equal mixture of irritation and relief. "I'm just never gonna cut it as a woman of mystery, am I? Okay, you win . . . I've known since last night but you'll hear it all on the ten o'clock news. Jason Saylin was murdered. Somebody fiddled strychnine into his coke. Happy?"

"Geez, Josh, don't be so bitter. I'm not trying to pump you. I married a lawyer, remember? I know all about keeping secrets. But there's only so much confidentiality one woman can stand . . . When I can't stand any more, I tell you because—"

Jocelyn finished the sentence for her. "—because you know I'll keep it to myself. Gotcha . . . and ditto. Here's the dirt . . ."

By the time the two women had made it over to Rockefeller Plaza to watch the skaters, Ruth was completely filled in on the Saylin killing. As they watched a svelte black man in a Brooks

Brothers suit making elaborate figure eights on the ice, Ruth observed, "They were a funny pair."

"Who? Jason and Courtney?"

"Hell, no. Courtney was a perfect Eva Braun to Jason's Hitler. I meant Jason and Andre. The social wed to the antisocial. After that time I dated him . . ."

"Dated who? *What* are you talking about, Ruth?"

"Didn't I ever tell you I went on a blind date with Andre Guérisseur? Oh, it was years ago. We had mutual friends . . . the Macklins set it up."

"No, Ruth, you *never* told me," she enunciated with slow precision so that each syllable could carry the full weight of her betrayed sensibilities. Her own reticence about Phillip and his work dwindled into nothingness in the face of such perfidy. Ruth, long accustomed to Jocelyn's fits of righteous indignation, threw back her head and hooted, "No, I guess I never did. It wasn't one of my dating triumphs. As a matter of fact, on a Richter scale of rejection, it was the San Francisco earthquake."

"You're kidding?! Why didn't you tell me?"

"Oh, listen, it was ages ago . . . before I met my Jake—the Zaftig Girl's Best Friend," Ruth said, comfortably patting her ample hips. "I was touchy back then . . . shoot, I was just plain devastated at the time."

"But what did he do? I can't imagine Andre being downright piggish."

"Oh, he wasn't! Not at all. That's what made it so awful. He was very attentive, very correct . . . and *very* revolted."

"Come on, Ruthie! Revolted?! You were a little heavier then but you still had the best bedroom eyes in Actors Equity."

"Big deal. With Andre the eyes do not have it. See, the Macklins are very dear people, but their notion of ideal matchmaking centers around pairing up people who are the same height, which Andre and I are—short! What they didn't realize is that Andre is adipose-phobic."

"Adipose-pho———? That's a *word?*"

"That's *my* word," Ruth said with a firm nod, "and I'm gonna write a monograph on it one day. It afflicts many people, but Andre Guérisseur has the most virulent case of it that I've ever come across. I remember we went to Regine's that night and it was chock full of models. He couldn't take his eyes off them . . . especially the tall ones who looked like borderline anorexics. In retrospect I think Andre sees himself as Dudley Moore in search of his Susan Anton . . . though even she might be a little too fleshy for his tastes. And lately I've often thought . . . aw, forget it. Let's go."

Ruth crossed the street and started heading for Radio City with Jocelyn hot on her heels.

"Thought what? I hate it when you don't finish a sentence."

"Golly, it's nothing, Josh. You know how I like to speculate about people. It's my favorite thing after Godiva chocolate. But you're meeting Phillip for dinner and the last thing either of you need right now is to be distracted by aimless speculation."

As always, what Ruth said made sense, but after years of practice Jocelyn was supersensitive to her friend's use of simple phrases like "golly" and "gosh." It usually meant that Ruth was hedging toward a devastatingly acute observation. Knowing that her only recourse was to bully, she reached out and grabbed the collar of Ruth's down coat, hauling her a good two inches off the pavement.

"Ruth, dear, I marched beside you in the No Nukes Rally this summer and you know how repugnant the idea of physical violence is to me, but if you don't tell me what you were thinking I'm going to pummel you with a pair of bunny feet!"

"Well, if you're going to take that attitude," Ruth sniffed, adjusting her collar with offended dignity, "I was just going to say . . . oh, gosh, it seems so silly . . . but I was just going to say that when I tried to think of all the women we knew who might come close to Andre's ideal, the person who always struck me as the strongest candidate was . . . Courtney Mason. I thought that way before Courtney got engaged to Saylin. I mean, she even has skinny *arms* . . . but it's dumb. It doesn't mean anything, Josh . . . Josh? You alright?"

But Jocelyn wasn't hearing Ruth's voice just then; she was hearing Andre Guérisseur saying, "I thought I'd be the one person she'd turn to now," and when Ruth's face finally forced its way back into her line of vision all she could do was whisper, "Oh, bloody hell."

CHAPTER IX

"Do you want some coffee?"

"No, thanks."

"How about dessert?"

"Unh-unh."

"Another drink maybe?"

"Nope."

"Well, Josh," Gerrard said, trying to keep the asperity out of his voice, "is there anything you *do* want?"

"Gee, I don't know . . . maybe a lawyer."

"For Christ's sakes!"

Phillip plucked the plastic swizzle stick from his drink and started mashing it into a tight little ball, while Jocelyn lit a cigarette and took a sip of her Pinot Chardonnay without interrupting her careful inspection of the tablecloth. The chicken *française* she'd just eaten wasn't sitting well with her, but it wasn't the chef's fault. She couldn't remember a meal this unpleasant since the time she came to the table wearing eye shadow in eighth grade. The fact that she was behaving just about as well now as she had then only made things worse; it pained her to regress in public. This wasn't supposed to happen after you hit thirty.

Phillip's train of thought was obviously running along the same tracks. Having reduced his swizzle stick to pulp, he leaned across the table and cupped her chin with one hand. "Look, before this all gets too Junior High and you decide to take another fellow to the Sock Hop, let me say that I'm sorry Irene's upset with you—"

"Upset?! You should have heard the message she left on my machine! I'm surprised the tape didn't shrivel—I sure did. She called me—among other things—a fascist stoolie!"

He wanted to laugh but didn't dare. Next week Jocelyn might see the humor in it but not tonight. Tonight she was feeling aggrieved and compromised; he could see it in the tight clench of her jaw and permitted himself only the smallest of smiles.

"What can I tell you? It goes with the territory. I don't think it hit Irene until today that she is actually a suspect in this case. She reacted the way most people would . . . a lot of outraged indignation spiced with paranoia. You remember—"

He stopped himself short, realizing what he was about to say and wanting to spare her an unwelcome reminder, but she'd already caught his drift.

"Oh, I remember alright," she grimaced wryly. "A vilely unique experience, that. Second only to my Aunt Milly's roast duck in downright fowl-ness."

"God, are you alright? You just made a pun, Josh. You *hate* puns."

"Ugh, you're right . . . But Phillip, that's just the trouble! I *do* know how Irene feels and how rotten it is. And even though I know you have your job to do . . . I just hate the idea of Irene thinking that I helped to put her in this position."

"I know you do," he said, catching both her hands in his and compelling her to look into his eyes, "I remember too, Josh. It's hell having to assemble and consider facts that are damning to someone you like. I've felt like that."

"You still do."

"Huh?"

"You didn't like hearing all that stuff Courtney said about Andre."

"I didn't say a thing when you told me about that," he protested.

"No, but you shredded your cocktail napkin," she said, staring pointedly at the small pile of confetti by his glass. "You always shred when you're unhappy. I understand, love. You like Andre and naturally hope he didn't do Jason in, and I feel the same way about Irene. But that doesn't alter the facts and right now they're both even money."

"Even? . . . How do you figure that? Come on, I know Ruth's a bright lady, but it's all conjecture on her part. If Andre was so hot for Courtney, why was he getting ready to clear out?"

"That could be a blind, Phillip," Jocelyn ventured mildly. She was working up to a hypothesis but wanted to spring it on him gently. "After all, the strongest thing against Irene right now is Saylin's pan. Andre might've read it before anyone got to the party. In retrospect, doesn't it strike you as a mite too Charlie Chan for life . . . that Andre just happened to be slipping that review into the drawer as we all came barging in? With that guilty flush on his face, it was bound to make people curious. He might have planned it all to throw suspicion on someone else . . . i.e., Irene."

His hand was itching to pick up Jocelyn's cocktail napkin and start tearing, but he checked himself and said, "You're good, O'Roarke. That's a slick piece of work and yes, it did cross my mind. But I still don't go for it. Jason and Andre, despite all appearances, weren't just employer and employee, they were *friends*. If Andre were really crazy enough about Courtney to kill for her, it would be a sudden crime, a crime of passion, not something so insidious as poisoning."

"Okay, Phillip, I see what you're getting at. But, admit it, your viewpoint is colored by what you know of Andre Guérisseur as a person. And maybe you're right. But I know Irene. Her temper is of the straw-fire variety . . . up with a whoosh but gone in a flash. Besides, she's gotten bad notices before now without ending up in the courts."

"But now's different, Josh. Now there's Marc."

"Marc? . . . I don't follow."

"She's more protective of him than she is of herself. I saw that today. She's nuts about him and, *Hedda* wasn't just another show to her—it was their baby, their joint creation. I know they've been together for a while, but Marc's younger than Irene and she probably worries about holding on to him. I think this show was especially important to her because it would link them together as a successful professional team as well as a couple. She wants his career to come to him through her. That makes her dangerous. I might be wrong but . . ." He stopped when he looked over and saw Jocelyn's hazel eyes brimming with tears.

"No, I don't think you're wrong," she sniffed, furious at the spectacle she was making, "not about Irene and Marc at least. But you know that through *me!* I natter on to you about my friends all the time . . . But it's so hard . . . I never meant it to hurt—" In danger of choking up completely, she belted back the last of her wine and regained a shred of composure. "God, I don't know what is the matter with me!"

"There's nothing the matter with you . . . nothing at all," he said, gently stroking her wrist and feeling like an ass. He was furious with himself for not fully appreciating the compromised position their relationship placed her in. It was true; she was one of his best sources of information on a case like this. Hopeless at remembering birthdays and anniversaries, Jocelyn was a gold mine of knowledge about theatre people, their past peccadilloes and present follies. She studied people the way a jeweler studies gems, critically but with enormous affection for their various facets. How could he forget that her shrewd, analytical mind was simply the protective coating for a kind and empathetic nature?

During the Weldon case it had been different; she was fighting to prove her own innocence then. But now, when there was no personal danger involved, she could only be helping to put a noose around someone else's neck. And she wasn't the old hand that he was with a knack for compartmentalizing people and evidence. It struck him suddenly, like an icy fist in the solar plexus, that—no matter what the outcome of this case—Jocelyn might well find the final consequences repugnant. He hoped mightily that that distaste might not spread to him and his job and contaminate their whole relationship. He drew small comfort from recalling Jocelyn's own observation that "nothing in life is germfree . . . nothing remotely interesting, that is." He knew that there was little in his power he could do to soften the shocks or make less harsh the demands that their intimacy would place on her.

What Gerrard wanted to do with a fierce desire, for just that evening, was to stuff his job in a hat and take Jocelyn off to see the Preston Sturges movie at the Regency, just to watch her laugh. What he had to do was to let her know that a hard time was about to get harder.

"There's nothing wrong with you, Josh . . . except maybe the guy you picked. I mean, I could give you the old cliché about 'it's a dirty job but somebody has to do it'—but that's bullshit. The fact is I *want* to do this job. It's what I'm good at and I believe in the function it fulfills. And, look, I know this sounds crazy, but if it's any comfort to you—most murderers *want* to be caught! Not the professionals, of course, but they're negligible. I mean the person who's weak enough to succumb to overwhelming circumstances and commit homicide. I knew a lawyer who once said that after the corpse, the second most devastated party was the killer. That kind of person has to be put away because he needs to be put away! They may not come right out and confess, but they can't live with the fact of their crime, either. It comes down to this—the act of killing breaks down the conventional boundaries of human behavior, and most people can't live without boundaries. It's too scary and too isolated. If they go undetected they'll do something else— something worse—to draw attention to themselves so that a higher authority—the law, in this case—will come in and reassert the old perimeters." Gerrard paused to catch his breath, then asked, "How am I doin'?"

"Not bad," Jocelyn said with a slow, appraising nod. Never before had she heard Phillip so passionately succinct about his work. "It's good psychology. I think you could prove a real threat to Dr. Joyce Brothers, and it has a sound basis in the classics."

"Huh? . . . Don't go artsy-fartsy on me now, Josh. I couldn't take it."

"I'm sorry. It's knee-jerk facetiousness. I was just thinking of a line from *Duchess of Malfi*—'Other sins only speak; murder shrieks out.' "

"Which means?"

"Which means," she said, "there's no room for niceties of distinction here . . . right? Either I help you or I don't. Either I tell you everything or nothing . . . right?"

Her eyes were full on him now, both forthright and questioning, and there was no way he could evade the issue. "That's right, Josh. I want your help . . . and I'll use whatever information you give me. And as much as I care for you . . ."

"Oh, give it a rest, Phillip. Spare me the 'I could not love thee, dear, so much/Lov'd I not honor more' part. I don't mean to mock or sound bitchy . . . because you're sincere and you're right. I'm ready to do the 'right thing' but I'm just not ready to feel great about it. Okay?"

"Fair 'nough," he said with a resigned nod. It wasn't quite the answer that he had hoped for, but it would have to do for the moment. There were other pressing matters at hand. In twenty minutes he was going to be questioning a key witness and he needed to get some information fast. Signaling the waiter for their check, he was aware of Jocelyn studying him with narrowed eyes through a cloud of cigarette smoke.

"There's just one more thing, Josh."

"Umm, I thought there might be," she said with an enigmatic smile.

"I want you to tell me everything you know about Franklin Allen."

She nodded, took a deep breath and quietly began shredding her cocktail napkin.

CHAPTER X

"Uh . . . Billy, dear fellow, could we go over that bit with the fan again because . . . as it stands now, it's a little bit lousy, you know."

"But, Franklin, I think it's gonna work. Know why?" The tall, thin actor in a period gown and wig crossed down to the apron of the stage, using the fan to accentuate his point. "See, I went to see Hoffman again in *Tootsie* and—"

But the director cut him short. "Oh, Tootsie-smootsie! Dustin's Dorothy is a purely contemporary woman. But Lady Bracknell is not an office girl! She's queen of all she surveys. That means you can't flap that fan around like a damn letter opener. Use it like a scepter. Use it to *rule*. Get it?"

A broad smile of comprehension creased the actor's face. "Oh, yeah, yeah . . . I see what you mean."

As the actor hiked up his skirts and resumed his place on stage, an aghast Tommy Zito, seated in the last row of the Above Boards Theatre, nudged his companion and whispered, "Phil, Phil, you see that? It's a *guy!* I thought it was . . . I mean I had no *idea* . . . Did you?"

"Yeah, I did. Josh told me. Allen's cashing in on the Golden Age of Theatrical Transsexuals with this production of *The Importance of Being Earnest.* Just breathe deep and brace yourself, son."

The scene picked up and ran to its end without a hitch. Franklin Allen summoned the company into the house and gave them his notes, which were terse and to the point but delivered with such lively wit and enthusiasm that, Gerrard could tell by looking at their faces, the actors left with a sense of a long day's work well done and better things in store. This was, Jocelyn had told him, Allen's great gift as a director: to cut to the heart of things without rending the vital organs. Clearly she hadn't been exaggerating, and

Phillip watched with keen interest as the small man with the shock of curly ginger hair made his way up the aisle looking like a preppy Woody Allen. He scanned the back of the house until he spotted the two policemen, then made a beeline over to them.

"Hello, Phillip. My assistant told me you were here. I was expecting it, of course. Good of you not to break in on rehearsal. It's hell to get their concentration back once it's been broken. And a murder investigation's just the thing to put them off their stride for sure. I hope I'm not being precipitous. It *is* a murder, isn't it?"

" 'Fraid so. But how did you know?"

"Oh, I didn't, not really. I missed this evening's news. But rumors run rampant and it's all the buzz. Would you both like to come up to my office? We can talk more privately there."

Franklin Allen's office was a study in controlled chaos. Scripts and papers abounded everywhere but were subdued into orderly stacks so as not to detract from the overall effect of theatrical flair and proud tradition. Posters from past productions hung on the walls alongside framed reviews—many of them Jason Saylin's, Phillip noticed. Small, sturdy plants lined the windowsills, nestled with various Drama Desk and Obie awards to create a subtle statement of long achievement. As he watched the diminutive director seat himself behind his desk, Phillip heard Jocelyn's words echo in his mind—"Gay as a goose and smart as a fox. It's a mistake ever to underestimate Franklin. For all his feyness, he usually knows *exactly* what he's doing."

"Now, gentlemen, what can I do you for," Allen asked, tilting his chair back at a precarious angle so that he could spray the plants on the sill behind him with a mister. "Don't let this stop you. Just time for me to do my Candide bit for the day—'cultivate our garden' and all that. It helps keep me sane vis-à-vis the vicissitudes of show business."

"Well, your fortunes certainly seem to be on the upswing these days, Mr. Allen," Gerrard replied artfully, suiting his voice and demeanor to the other man's air of careful urbanity.

"Oh, please—make it Franklin. After all, we are acquainted through mutual . . . friends," he said with the smallest of twinkles in his eyes. "But, yes, you're right, Phillip. If you're referring to

Hedda, it's doing quite nicely at the box office . . . for the moment anyway."

"Any reason why that should change?"

Allen gave a sly chuckle as he pinched a dead leaf from a coleus. "Now you're being cunning with me, aren't you? This is better than *Columbo* reruns! But to come to the point, I'd venture to say that the future health and long life of *Hedda Gabler* depends on whether the papers print Jason's review. Wouldn't you?"

"Ah . . . you've spoken to Miss Ingersoll, I take it," Gerrard asked easily, giving no sign of his consternation at Allen's aplomb.

"Yes, indeed. Though, to be accurate, she did most of the speaking." The twinkle was growing. "I must say you seem to have a remarkable effect on actresses. She was in a rare state on the phone—even for Irenie. Accused me of all sorts of things . . . happily, murder was not amongst them. She seems to have gotten it into her head that I had *promised* her a good review from Saylin!"

"Now I wonder how she got that impression?"

To the amazement of the two policemen, the tiny man threw back his head and guffawed. "God, you're too good! . . . Really perfect . . . Oh, oh, excuse me. This is unforgiveable." He paused to wipe tears of mirth from his eyes. "But truly . . . you do it so well. Makes me want to do an Agatha Christie play. I don't suppose you've ever considered—"

His question was cut short when he encountered Gerrard's implacable gaze. Hardened criminals had quaked under its scrutiny and Franklin was no exception. He got himself under control in short order.

"About that review, Franklin?"

"Yes, yes . . . the review. Of course, I *never* promised Irene a good notice from Jason. How could I? Oh, I'm not saying that it's never been done . . . that there aren't ways. There've been critics on the take before . . . and producers who would stoop to bribery. But not Jason. Others have tried and failed dismally and I would never think of trying. It's vanity, you see . . . I think I'm pretty good. Jason seemed to think so, too. He was usually keen on me in his reviews. Even his first review of *Hedda* only attacked Irene, not the production."

"So why were you so sure his second review would be any kinder to her?"

"Oh, well, there were several reasons," he murmured as he picked up a steel pen and began twirling it through his fingers.

"Care to run them by me?"

"They're pretty obvious, really. Despite his first notice, we did quite well in the Off-Broadway run. If we hadn't we would've never made the move. And everybody loves a winner—even critics, though they don't admit it. That's for starters. Secondly, I think Jason realized that his own particular bias had affected his critique of Irene's performance."

"What bias is that?"

The director threw his hands up in exasperation. "Everybody *knows!* Saylin had a thing about perfect women. Good lord, man, if you read that first review you must know that the biggest thing he had against Irene was her physical *size!* It was her waistline, not her acting, that he took issue with. But the public—God love 'em— aren't so particular. The audience *loves* her in that part. He never outright admitted it to me but I'm sure it made him think twice."

"Even after Irene dumped a plate of pasta on his head? That strikes me as incredibly broad-minded of him. You sure Irene's little threat about exposing his cocaine habit had *nothing* to do with it?"

Allen froze in his seat and took a long pause before replying, while Phillip studied him for signs of disintegration. It was a fruitless search, and he had an unaccountable feeling that he had, instead of delivering a coup de grace, just played into the other man's hand. Finally Franklin gave his answer.

"No, definitely not. I told Irene at the time that pulling a stunt like that could backfire on us with devastating effect. I don't bribe and I don't threaten. Besides, we didn't need to."

"How could you be so sure?"

It was a question begging to be asked but, as a slow smile spread across Franklin Allen's face, Phillip realized that it was the one he had been waiting for.

"Because, you see . . . and I know this is going to sound shocking . . . I'd already been approached through various discreet channels with the offer of fresh backing from a new investor . . .

'angels,' we call 'em. It's all a little tricky and circuitous when you see it on paper, but there was no question at all that the person wearing the wings in this instance was none other than Jason Saylin himself."

CHAPTER XI

"This is just dandy . . . a fine kettle of fish! Stopped dating actors, started dating a cop. See where it's got you? Out of the frying pan and into the friggin' fire!"

Jocelyn had been muttering to herself for some minutes as she wended her way up Broadway toward her apartment after leaving the restaurant. It wasn't until she noticed passersby giving her the kind of guardedly pitying glance normally reserved for bag-ladies that she realized it was time to get a grip on herself. Going home wasn't the answer—there was nothing left to clean. She'd just fret about Irene and put off calling Andre. That was it—Andre! Now maybe there she could *do* something.

Dodging traffic with the nimbleness of a quarterback, she made it to an available phone booth and started dialing feverishly, making a conscious effort to slow her breathing down lest she sound over eager. Luckily the phone rang five times before someone picked it up.

"Hello."

"Hi . . . Andre, that you? This is Jocelyn O'Roarke."

"J-Jocelyn, I'm glad it's you. I've been waiting for your call."

"Yes, I know. Sorry to get back to you so late. I've been on the go all day. But, listen, I saw Courtney and I'm in the neighborhood right now," she fibbed. "Would it be okay if I dropped in to give you the news?"

"Why s-sure. How soon should I expect you?"

"Oh, about five minutes say. See you in a bit."

She was hailing a cab even as her other hand replaced the receiver. A Checker came promptly to heel and she bolted inside, snapping out, "Central Park West and Sixty-first, please," barely holding back an "and make it snappy." It wouldn't do to give in to her Bogart fantasies this early in the evening. Much better to stick to the Mary Astor approach for the time being.

It was more than a little eerie stepping back into Saylin's apartment again. All signs of police activity had vanished, but the cream-colored carpet and thirties furniture had a mausoleum tinge to them tonight. This effect was enhanced by the packing crates stuck discreetly in corners of the room, and Guérisseur's mien, reminiscent of a doleful caretaker.

"Excuse the m-mess, Jocelyn. I just can't seem to keep still for more than two minutes . . . must be my way of coping with sh-shock. After I finished making the funeral arrangements—I thought I'd best not to wait on C-Courtney—I decided to get some packing done. I'm m-moving soon, you see."

"Yes, I . . . uh . . . heard."

"Oh, did she . . . Courtney tell you? What did she say? How is she?" The stutter disappeared as his voice became more animated, but he held himself with a certain awkward tension as if he were prepared to flinch. Jocelyn's chicken *française* did a queasy somersault in her stomach as it dawned on her that, in her anxiousness to play Girl Detective, she had completely overlooked the fact that Andre would want all the gruesome details of her harrowing interview with Courtney . . . and she hadn't yet decided on the best way of editing that unpleasant script.

"Gee, Andre, give me a minute to collect myself. Like I said, it's been a busy day and I'm all in. Do you have anything to drink handy?"

It was a good ploy, especially with someone as conscientiously well mannered as Andre. He flushed and stammered, "F-Forgive me, Jocelyn. I'm being rude. I've just put some coffee on. Would you like that or something s-stronger?"

"Coffee would be fine, thanks."

"Good. Why don't you settle yourself in the living room and I'll be b-back in a jiffy," he said already trundling off toward the kitchen.

She took a roundabout path to the mauve velvet sofa in order to peek inside various open cartons on the floor. Most of them contained books on theatre and literature, but one slim volume caught her eye. It read *"Lost Ladies: Forgotten Women in Films* by Andre Guérisseur." She was about to pluck it out of the box, but the sound of footsteps made her bolt for the sofa. When Andre entered the room carrying a glass tray with matching cups and saucers, she was lounging against the cushions, leisurely smoking a cigarette.

As it turned out, there *was* nothing stronger than Guérisseur's coffee. Jocelyn had tasted nothing like it since the death of her Irish grandfather, who had once been a galley boy in the merchant marines and used to concoct a similar potion which she and her brothers had dubbed "Elephant's Brew." She had no idea how Andre had gotten the recipe, but she was grateful for its powerful effects. She needed her wits about her. However, having discharged his duties as a host, Andre barely allowed her two sips before resuming his inquiries.

"So, how is C-Courtney, Josh? I don't mean to press but I've been so worried. I spoke with Patsy once today but she was rather . . . brief. I don't think she likes me."

"Oh, don't worry about that. Patsy affects not to like anybody. That's how she gets people to fall all over her. It's just her way of doing business. Pay no heed."

"Yes, yes, I see but . . ."

"Yes, about Courtney . . . I don't know what to tell you, except that I think you were wise to go ahead with making the arrangements. She's still on medication and not ready to really face up to the fact of Jason's death. Actually she talked more about their wedding plans than anything . . ."

"Oh, the poor girl, the poor, poor girl. It's all too cruel and she's so d-delicate," he murmured. His head was hung low, so all she could see was his balding pate, but even that looked miserable. She fidgeted beside him on the sofa, wishing she could pat his hunched shoulders and say something suitably consoling. But ingrained pragmatism won out over finer feelings.

"Hey, look, Andre. She's having a mini-breakdown, that's all. Under the circumstances that's pretty par for the course. She'll bounce back when she's good and ready. I don't mean to sound crude, but you shouldn't over romanticize all this. Her people got through the Civil War and the Reconstruction. Southern women are aces at rising from the ashes. 'Iron Magnolia' is no idle phrase, you know."

Her words brought Guérisseur out of his slump but not in the way she had hoped. He jumped off the sofa and began pacing the room with a fury.

"No, no, you're wrong! You don't know her. She's terribly sensitive. I know you're her f-friend, but you don't know her like I . . . you just don't *know!* Jason was everything to her. It wasn't just that she loved him. He was her hope, her future—*everything!* She's not like you. When she met Jason, she'd been working in New York for ten years, but her talent was never recognized or a-appreciated. She was ready to p-pack it in . . . go back home. Even though she loves the theatre and being here. With Jason she had a reason to s-stay. He made her feel part of things again and v-valuable. All that's taken away from her now. She's all a-alone now."

"So why are you leaving?" It was a rotten thing to ask, but dating Phillip had taught her that nice questions got you nowhere. Andre stopped pacing and collapsed in an easy chair.

"I h-have to. I've already made a commitment . . . signed a contract before all this happened. I have to go now."

"But you didn't *have* to go before you decided to take this job. What prompted you?"

He raised his head to look at her and, despite his agitation, a certain wariness came into his eyes. "She told you about it, didn't she? About my taking this teaching job? I know she wasn't h-happy about it. What did she s-say?"

"Uh . . . she seemed to find it a little inexplicable," Jocelyn replied smoothly, mentally granting herself the Understatement of the Year Award. "Seemed to feel you were leaving Jason in the lurch a bit."

"I know, I know she did. But it was for the best," he said, extending his hands forward in a supplicating gesture. "I couldn't go on living here after they were m-married. And for a long time now I've wanted to teach and do . . . other th-things."

"Like write?"

"What makes you say that?"

"Well, I noticed your book in one of the boxes. I didn't know you were a published author."

"Oh, that," he said with a dismissive shrug. "That's nothing. Something that I started when I was still in c-college. Flipper—uh, Phillip can tell you. I was a big movie buff then, and I got fascinated with all these women—w-wonderful actresses like Mae Murray and Nita Naldi—who got lost in the Hollywood shuffle, so I wrote the b-book. My father had some contacts in publishing back then so it got printed . . . and quickly forgotten, except by my m-mother, of course."

"I'd like to read it sometime. I only saw Nita Naldi in one picture but I loved her."

"Well, you might find it interesting then." He was more relaxed now that they were on safer ground. "I had a spare copy but Jason lent it to someone. I don't know who. I guess now there's no hope of getting it b-back." To Jocelyn's dismay his eyes suddenly filled with tears. "Oh, God, Jason . . . Jason, he was *so* unlucky."

Despite his violent demise, Jocelyn couldn't quite see what had been so unlucky in Saylin's life, but before she could find a tactful way of framing that question Andre rose from his seat, rubbing his face with both hands, and said, "Sorry, Jocelyn. I didn't mean to put you through all th-this. I guess the strain is finally beginning to take its toll on me. Do you mind if we call it a n-night?"

"No, not at all," she lied. She would've liked to stay and get Andre Guérisseur roaring drunk, because she had a sure hunch that there was a lot more he could tell her. But she was helpless in the face of his abject sadness, so she put the best face on it that she could muster and said, "I've stayed too long as it is. You need some rest."

Ever the gentleman, he escorted her to the door, where they stood making awkward small talk until Jocelyn spied something poking out of one of the open crates.

"Why, Andre, what a lovely old cane! It's hickory wood, isn't it?"

"Oh, yes, it's a fine piece—quite rare. At least that one is . . . one of a pair. Courtney found them in New Orleans last summer and bought the set for Jason and me . . . to celebrate the engagement. It was the first gift she ever g-gave me," he said, caressing the fine wood with such forlorn tenderness that she had to avert her eyes, feeling that she had no right to witness such a private moment.

Once out in the hall she bolted for the elevator which, when it arrived, was mercifully empty. Stepping inside she leaned her head against the cushioned walls and waited for the hot flush to leave her cheeks. She was blushing—not from embarrassment at Andre's display of feeling, but from a sense of shame. What right had she to go traipsing around like an over-the-hill Nancy Drew? Who was she to insinuate herself into people's personal tragedies under false pretenses, merely to satisfy her own curiosity, when there was nothing to be gained from it? Clearly she was out of her depths here, and if there was anything she despised it was a dilettante.

She went on like this, mentally flagellating herself as only an ex-Catholic can, down all fourteen floors to the lobby. When she hit the sidewalk and began walking home, the bracing night air did much to restore her equilibrium, as did one of Ruth Bernstein's favorite Yiddish bromides—"So call me *pisher.*" Well, a *pisher* I am, she thought, and a *pisher* I'll probably stay. But I learned one thing tonight for whatever it's worth. Ruthie's hunch was right. Andre's in love with Courtney. He's as far gone as I've ever seen a man over a woman.

Despite the odds against him—Courtney's engagement to Jason, her obvious distaste for the man and Andre's own self-effacement—he was the epitome of "Love, bumping his head blindly against all the obstacles of civilization."

CHAPTER XII

"A little higher, Tommy . . . yeah, right there. Oh God, that feels good."

In the privacy of Phillip Gerrard's office, Tommy Zito was giving his boss a morning neck rub. A big self-improvement buff, Zito had once taken a night course in massage therapy which had uncovered a hidden talent and made him a very popular fellow in the precinct house. Right now his short, meaty fingers were bringing magical relief to a tight knot in Phillip's left shoulder, caused by a night of fruitless speculation over his surprising interview with Franklin Allen.

Sighing contentedly, Gerrard let his head sink lower in order to take a sip of *café con leche* from the container on his desk and said, "So, what've we got? A dead critic who pans a show then offers to back it. Makes *no* sense . . . unless Franklin knows more than he's telling. Which he probably does but isn't about to tell us, not right away. Time to get back to hard facts. What've the lab boys got for us?"

Tommy's hands froze briefly then began their kneading motions with renewed vigor. "A little . . . but not as much as we'd hoped for."

"What the hell does that mean?"

"Easy, Phil. You're tensing. Well, your hunch about the terrace was right. There was strychnine out there. They had a sack of Mouse Maze. It's a common rodenticide and it's loaded with the stuff. But we don't know if it matches with the poison in the cocaine vial . . . yet."

"*Yet!* They've had it for twenty-four hours! Mr. Wizard could teach a five year old to do the analysis in that time."

"I know, I know," Tommy said miserably, feeling all his therapeutic efforts slip away as Gerrard's back muscles assumed the consistency of dry cement. "There was a screwup in the lab. They've gotta do the tests over."

"Jesus H. Christ!" Phillip violently uprighted himself in his chair, sending Zito careening back into a file cabinet. "That means we're still stuck with half of Manhattan as possible suspects!"

"Hey, come on, Phil," Tommy said, rubbing a bruised elbow. "It's not as bad as that. I mean, it's still a pretty good guess that whoever knocked off Saylin didn't come to the party with a package of strychnine in their pocket. How could anybody know that he was gonna be throwin' his snow around like confetti that night?"

"So you think someone saw a golden opportunity and seized it, huh?" Phillip thoughtfully picked up the cut-glass vial on his desk and studied the delicate engraving on the silver top. It read "To J.S. from C."—just as its twin did. "Well, that might narrow things down a bit. After all, not everyone at the party got a tour of the greenhouse. Care to make any guesses?"

Tommy slowly edged his way around to the front of the desk, head tilted to one side as he scratched his neck. Gerrard instantly recognized this as his "reluctant pose," which he always assumed just as he was ready to plump for his favorite suspect.

"Well, I was thinkin', ya know . . . The only person we know for sure who saw that bum notice is Carson . . . and he didn't tell us right off. He only admitted it when you were closing in on Miss Ingersoll . . . and her I believed! I don't think she knew a damn thing about that review. She was too surprised."

"Tommy, she's an actress and a good one . . ."

"Yeah, but she's also Carson's meal ticket. I mean, maybe he loves her, maybe he don't. But it's plain as day his career won't amount to bupkis without her. So, I've been doin' some checking up on him."

"What did you come up with?"

"Well, it's not hard evidence . . . And I guess we coulda got it from Jocelyn in a minute, but I woulda felt a little crummy asking her," Tommy said easily, unaware that he had just stuck a dagger in his friend's heart. "But I found out that Carson, when he was a college kid, had a steady job four summers running . . . with an exterminating company. He'd recognize a bag of Mouse Maze from twenty paces, easy. Whad ya think?"

"I think that's pretty interesting, but there's something else we have to consider," Phillip said, grimly crushing his coffee container with his right hand. "I happen to know—via Jocelyn, unfortunately —that Irene Ingersoll grew up on a farm in Wisconsin. Her father grew corn and, in her girlhood days, Irene killed more rats than you could shake a stick at. So where does that leave us?"

The two men stared at each other across the desk in a melancholy stalemate until there was a knock at the door. Detective Jerry Fallon breezed into the room, fresh from his morning jog and oblivious to the constrained silence around him.

Fallon, who had attended City College and secretly considered himself a more fit partner for the precinct's chief detective than any Italian butcher's son from Brooklyn, dropped a typewritten list on Gerrard's desk with ill-concealed smugness.

"Thought you'd want to see this, Phil. It has to do with that drug homicide you were working on before the Saylin case came up. Like we thought, the guy was just some penny-ante courier who got nailed on his delivery route. We found a list of addresses on him and I thought you might like to take a gander. Looks like it was his roster for that night."

While Phillip scanned the list, Fallon perched himself on the corner of the desk, perfectly blocking Tommy's view of the paper. With feigned placidity, Zito leaned back in his seat and slowly and methodically began cracking each of his knuckles. It wasn't what he really wanted to be doing with his knuckles, but it had its effect. By the time Gerrard slid the sheet across to him, Fallon was up and edging toward the door, wiping his palms on the back of his tan slacks.

"Well, Phil, I don't know if that's any help. Just wanted to let you know."

"Yeah, sure, Jerry. Thanks. Keep me posted if you come up with anything else, okay?"

"Sure thing, yeah. And if you need any extra help . . . I'm always here. See ya."

The door clicked shut and, after muttering some choice Italian curses under his breath, Zito was getting ready to seriously study the list when he noticed that his chief was quietly chuckling.

"What's so funny?"

"Oh, nothing. I was just thinking of something Josh said when she met Fallon."

"Where'd she meet that twerp?"

"We ran into him one Sunday in the Park while he was jogging. Afterward Josh said he reminded her of an understudy she knew once—'ambition seething in the wings' was her phrase."

"Hey, that's pretty good. I like that," Tommy said, brightening visibly. "Really hits the nail on the friggin' head. She's one smart broad . . . uh, lady."

In a happier frame of mind Zito began studying the sheet in his hand. It was nothing but a list of various addresses in Manhattan—no names attached, just different times penciled in next to each entry. Halfway down the page was a by now familiar address on Central Park West with the time "ten P.M." written along side it.

"Geez, that's Saylin's place, huh? He was gonna score some more coke that night. That's pretty ballsy, seein' how he knew you'd be at the party. What a nerve on that guy!"

"But he didn't know at the time. Andre invited us at the last minute. I guess that's why he was less than thrilled to see me there. As it turns out, he had nothing to worry about. His delivery boy was dead and cold in the East Village by six o'clock."

"But the way he was tossin' his blow around that night—he didn't know that."

"No, *he* didn't," Gerrard said thoughtfully, "but maybe somebody else did."

CHAPTER XIII

"For those of you who haven't been listening, I repeat—There is no Evelyn Wood School of Acting. There are no short cuts. It's a process. It's not magic. You can't do eight shows a week on magic! Sometimes you feel like doing it and sometimes you don't, but you have to do it anyway. That's why feeling isn't enough. Emotion without technique is like tomato sauce without pasta—a runny mess. So when you bring your scenes in next week, you bring costumes, props *and* blocking. Capisce? Good. That's it for today, everybody."

To Jocelyn's surprise, a small burst of applause once again greeted her final spate of harassment. A twenty-year-old garage mechanic from the Bronx, who had done a credible Stanley Kowalski that day, gave her a playful shot in the arm and grinned down at her, saying, "Way to go, coach," on his way out.

Tidying up her small classroom on the top floor of the Cubiculo Theatre, she felt the way she always did after teaching a class—exhausted, happy and more than a little humble. It still amazed her that she could earn money by showing people how to profit from *her* mistakes. That, in her view, was her most valuable asset as a teacher; she had made *all* the mistakes . . . and lived to tell about them.

Little did her students know that, on days like this, she felt like paying them for the therapeutic joy of teaching. For five whole hours she got to concentrate on something she loved—actors and their work—without once thinking of Jason Saylin and his faceless killer. It was a relief.

But the relief was short-lived. A painful reminder was waiting four flights down in the person of Patsy Snell. Seated on a bench in the lobby, wearing a bomber jacket and denim skirt, Patsy was conferring with a young director who was preparing to mount the latest "definitive" Vietnam play. Putting two fingers in her mouth, she whistled a short, sharp note to attract Jocelyn's attention and rose from the bench, saying, "Yeah, I get the idea . . . napalm lighting. I know what you want, Jack-o. I also know what you can *afford.* When you find the backing, give me a call. Hey, O'Roarke, wait up."

Wanting nothing but a swim and a long steam, Jocelyn reluctantly let go of the door handle and turned to face the older woman.

"Hi, Patsy. How're things going? Courtney feeling any better?"

"No, she's not. She's feeling a hell of a lot worse, as a matter of fact. That's why I want to talk to you."

Taking no notice of Jocelyn's feeble protest, she grabbed her elbow and steered her out the door and around the corner to LaPalma, a Cuban-Asian restaurant whose food was as good as its wallpaper was bad. If the food were in keeping with the decor, every entree would arrive gilded in aluminum foil. But such was not the case, and Jocelyn felt somewhat recompensed for missing her health club when two Dos Equis and a plate of shrimp in garlic sauce were placed on the table. Patsy got down to the food and her point without preliminaries.

"I'm worried about Court. She's not well."

"Patsy, what do you expect? She's had an awful blow."

"No, that's not what I mean . . . not just her mental state. She's physically not well. She's in no condition to even attend the funeral tomorrow. I don't know what to do about it and it's making me damn crazy. I thought you should know—"

"Me?! Why me? Why not call her family?"

"Unh-unh. She won't hear of it. That'd put her over the edge for sure. But I've gotta tell somebody."

"Alright, but Patsy, not *me!* I mean, whatever it is there's very little I can do to help . . . and you know who I'm involved with. I can't even promise you confidentiality. Do you want this to get back to the police?"

"Christ! Yes, maybe I do . . . though I don't see how it can figure in with Jason's death. All I know is that I don't want the responsibility. I'm passing the buck here, O'Roarke, and you're the only person I can think of passing it to. So, here goes. Ever since she's been back at the apartment, she's been puking her guts up at the drop of a hat. I called the doctor in this morning to take a look at her. She screamed bloody murder but I wasn't listening. He gave her a real going-over, took urine and blood samples, then left. He didn't say much, but I could see which way the wind was blowing. I think she's pregnant and, as a matter of hellish fact, so does she. Seems she's thought so for a while but was too afraid to say anything."

"Oh, God, that is rough. No wonder she's so whacked out. And all those pills and wine. She shouldn't be near that stuff."

"Skip the prenatal care. What I want to know is, has Jason provided for her in his will or not?"

"His will? I don't have any idea. I know his parents are both dead and he has no close relatives . . . and he had a trust fund. But as far as what provisions he made, I haven't a clue . . . though it does seem likely that the bulk of it would go to Courtney and Andre."

"Well, I hope to hell you're right."

"Why? Does she need the money that bad? Oh, crap, that's a silly question, isn't it. Anybody with a kid needs money. But, anyway, Patsy, no matter how the estate falls out, at least when all this is over, she'll have some consolation. She'll have Jason's child."

"Back up, cookie. You're two steps ahead of the story line. Before I left the apartment this morning, she told me in no uncertain terms that, if it turns out she is knocked up, she intends to have an abortion . . . and no two ways about it."

Ninety minutes later Jocelyn finally reached her health club, after having mollified Patsy with several more Dos Equis and the promise that she would try to find out what she could about Saylin's last will and testament. True to her word, she resisted the siren call of the lap lane and made her way over to the pay phone to call Phillip.

"Jocelyn, hi! Where the hell've you been? I called last night when I got through with Allen but you weren't in."

"Oh, yeah. I paid a little visit on my way home. I'll tell you about it later. Why don't you come up to my place for dinner? I'll make teriyaki."

"You bet I will. What've you been up to, O'Roarke? You only cook Japanese when you're feeling guilty."

"Goddamn it, Phillip! If you're going to question my every—"

"Ah, ah, cool your jets, missy. You can tell me all about it to-night. I'm sure a few glasses of saki will restore your usually benign and candid nature. But am I right in assuming that this call is prompted by something more than your desire to dazzle me with your culinary skills?"

"Yes, Great Oz, it is," she said, vexed with her own transparency. "Right now, *I* need a little information. Have you heard anything yet about Saylin's will as far as who inherits and to the tune of how much?"

"No, not yet. His lawyers are being a little shirty about divulging, but they'll come through in a day or so. Who wants to know, Josh?" All the playfulness was gone from his voice and things were clearly on a back-to-business basis, so Jocelyn gave him a quick summary of her meeting with Patsy Snell and her news about Courtney.

"It's just that Patsy's so worried about Courtney and this talk about getting an abortion . . . It's not like her. Courtney's sophis-tication goes no deeper than her foundation base. At heart she's a good Southern Baptist girl, grounded in the virtues of home and hearth. That's why Patsy thought if there was money coming to her, it might make a difference."

"I doubt that seriously. I don't think inheriting Jason's money is going to make any difference."

"Why?" she asked, puzzled by the sudden coldness of his tone.

Gerrard took a long minute before replying. "Josh, remember I told you that Jason had more than his share of luck with the ladies when we were in college?"

"Yeah, so?"

"Well, in certain quarters, he was popular for more than his boyish charm. I . . . uh . . . dated a girl at one point—hell, *ev-erybody* dated her at one point, and I would appreciate not having this thrown in my face at a later time—anyway, this girl loved sex but hated rubbers. Jason was one of her favorite beauxs because, as she put it, 'there was no muss and no fuss.' "

"Meaning?"

"Meaning that, according to her, he had contracted mumps at a dangerous age for a man. Jason Saylin was sterile."

CHAPTER XIV

"Now, cut that out," Jocelyn said in her best Jack Benny voice. "If I pour some soy sauce on your Kal Kan *then* will you eat it?"

Completely ignoring the meal set before him, Angus was making violent figure eights around her ankles in the hopes of procuring a slice of flank steak before it went into the wok. Mildly irritating as it was, Jocelyn welcomed the distraction. It kept her from stewing over recent events and the possible paternity of Courtney Mason's child. But she was no match for Angus's feline footwork and, after slipping him a cube of meat, she was free to stir-fry and stew at the same time.

In terms of proximity, Andre Guérisseur seemed the likeliest candidate for Bachelor Father. But, considering his air of terminal unrequitedness and Courtney's obvious detestation of the man, the idea seemed ludicrous. In the days before Saylin, Courtney had dated around quite a bit, and Jocelyn was trying to dredge her memory for the names of old flames when the phone rang. She turned the burner off and crossed to the phone, hoping that it wasn't Phillip calling to say that he'd been held up at the lab. She knew how anxious he was to get that report on the strychnine, but revitalizing cold teriyaki was beyond her kitchen arts. The voice at the other end sounded harried, but it didn't belong to one of New York's Finest.

"Jocelyn. Franklin Allen here. Listen, have you heard from Irene today?"

"No, Franklin, I haven't," she said, neglecting to mention that according to Irene their next chat wasn't scheduled until Dante's Inferno opened a skating rink. "Why? What's up?"

"Oh, nothing much," he said with acrid archness, "except that we happen to be into half hour here and our Hedda has not yet deigned to show her face. The silly bitch!"

Jocelyn glanced down at her watch and saw that it was, indeed, seven-thirty. "That's not like her. Irene likes to flirt for an hour with the stagehands before a show. Have you called her apartment?"

"Of *course* I have! Marc answered. He'd just gotten in. Apparently they had some stupid fight this morning and she stormed out to God knows where. Probably a bar, blast her!"

"Well, if I were you, I'd try Jimmy Ray's. That's her favorite hangout. But she'd have to be pretty upset to drink before a show. Did Marc say what the fight was about?"

"Yes, naturally." Allen broke away from the phone to send his assistant stage manager hightailing over to Jimmy Ray's, then came back. "Marc tells me everything—I've been like a father to that boy—and what do I get for it?! I would *love*, really adore, to know why straight people take their sex so seriously."

"Franklin, hold on. I know you're on a roll, but I haven't the faintest idea what you're talking about. Why did they fight?"

"Oh, that, yes . . . that's what I mean, so silly, so trivial. Marc got a call this morning from La Mason. Obviously, she was in need of some high-level hand-holding. She asked Marc to meet her for lunch. That's when Irene developed her China Syndrome."

"Courtney called *Marc?* But why?"

"My dear, are you getting senile or has monogamy dulled your senses? They're old pals from modeling days—the quintessential 'just good friends' relationship. I don't know if they were ever lovers, but Irene obviously has her own opinions on the subject. That vixen! Doesn't she know that Ibsen is worth any three men rolled together? And we're sold-out tonight! Damn all actresses—excuse me, Jocelyn—but damn their libidinous little souls to hell, that's all I can say. Well, I'd better go throw some cold water on Irene's understudy. She was looking awfully peaked at half hour. Let me know if Irene gets in touch with you . . . so I can strangle her. Bye now."

Jocelyn slammed down the receiver and stared angrily at the offending instrument, muttering, "Who the hell do these people think I am—Mary Worth?!" Shaking herself, she strode purposefully back to the stove to resume her preparations, reminding herself that Franklin always said outrageous things when he was crossed. So Marc and Courtney were old acquaintances—so what, she thought. It didn't necessarily mean anything; Franklin was just repeating gossip. But gossip, as her old Latin teacher was wont to quote, is "light and easy to raise, but grievous to bear and hard to get rid of" . . . impossible, for Jocelyn in this instance. After taking a few ineffectual pokes at the flank steak, she flicked off the burner again and crossed back to the phone, hating, as always, those moments in life when nuns are proven right.

Marc Carson picked up before the second ring.

"Hello . . . Irene, is that you?"

"Guess again, fella. It's Jocelyn."

"Oh, Josh, hi . . . You haven't heard from Irene by any chance, have you?"

"Not bloody likely. You know damn well that in her book I'm currently listed as persona non existo. I've heard from Allen though. He's a mite peeved."

"Well . . . uh . . . so you know, then?"

If he hadn't sounded so much like a shamefaced schoolboy, she might have exercised some forbearance. Instead she snapped, "No, I don't *know* anything! I just hear things. Within the last forty-eight hours I have become a cornucopia of vague innuendos and it's getting on my nerves. Why didn't you tell Phillip that you were friends with Courtney?"

"Tell Phillip! Is he with you now?"

"No, you jackass, he's not. But he will be in a minute. That's why I'm calling. Don't you realize how bad it looks to withhold that kind of information?!"

"But, Josh, I just didn't think. It's such a small thing . . ."

"Not anymore it's not, you cretin. This is a murder investigation. You don't get to decide on proportions. And, if you're clean, you don't fart around with the police. Now . . . What're you gonna do?"

"Goddamned if I know. You're right, I realize that, but I'm so confused now. And I'm worried sick about Irene. I just can't think . . . Listen, can I meet with you tomorrow? I know it's a lot to ask, but I'd like you to hear my side of things . . . before I go to Gerrard."

"Marc . . . it's not going to make any difference—"

"I know, yes, but, please, Josh—for old times' sake. I need some-body to help me sort things out. Please?"

Cursing herself for an interfering fool, she made a date to meet him at the Metropolitan Museum for lunch and agreed not to mention anything to Phillip in the meantime. It was all wrong and she knew it, but aside from the ties of friendship, she felt sure that she could get more out of Marc than would be gained from a tense cross-examination at the police station.

Five minutes later, when Phillip buzzed her apartment, the ter-iyaki was almost ready but Jocelyn wasn't. She hadn't had sufficient time to come to terms with her duplicity. One look at his harried appearance and the dark shadows under his fine gray eyes made her feel like Judas Iscariot's last surviving relative. But she'd given Marc her word and it was too late to go back on it.

Taking a bottle of saki out of a paper bag, Phillip placed it on the counter, tossed the crumpled bag into the fireplace and came over to Jocelyn, greeting her with an embrace that belied his apparent fatigue. When they finally broke apart, he placed a finger on her lips and said, "What I would like more than anything, Josh, is a nice, quiet meal with *no* shop talk. Do you think we can swing it?"

"No sweat, sarge. We can play Hits from the Past—if you're up to it."

"You're on, O'Roarke."

With the teriyaki on the table and Gato Barbieri on the stereo, they settled down to a round of Jocelyn's only contribution to the world of parlor games. Hits from the Past was a master stroke of facetiousness born of desperation. Laboring under a spectacularly boring history professor in college, Jocelyn had discovered that the only way she could stay awake during his endless lectures at eight in the morning was to think up famous figures singing their "hit" tune. During a tedious dissertation on the French Revolution, she had come up with Marie Antoinette singing "Goin' Out of My Head" and Jean-Paul Marat singing "Splish Splash, I Was Takin' a Bath." A campus craze had been born.

After knowing Jocelyn for nearly a year, Phillip had become adept at the game and had expanded the repertoire to include well-known fictional characters. Taking a ruminative sip of his iced saki, he started the ball rolling with Count Dracula singing "Peg o' My

Heart." Jocelyn gagged on her rice but came back with Quasimodo singing "Bells Are Ringing." At one point she surged ahead with the Marquis de Sade singing "You Only Hurt the One You Love" and Lucretia Borgia doing "How Does the Wine Taste?" But Phillip capped the round and the meal when he hit on Catherine the Great singing "I've Got the Horse Right Here," and Jocelyn slid under the table in convulsions.

But by the time she brought two mugs of decaf espresso over to the sofa, Jocelyn saw that Play Hour was just about over. Despite a lingering smile, there was a certain flintiness coming into those gray eyes that, she knew from past experience, meant business. Handing him his mug, she was much surprised when he unexpectedly pulled her down beside him and gave her a long, ardent kiss. Coming up for air, she gasped, "Why, Cap'n Butler—what *are* you doin'?"

"Just reminding both of us of a basic fact—that I'm pretty crazy about you, O'Roarke," he said in a voice that was both brusque and heated.

"Well, I'm grateful for the reminder . . . but why are you suddenly sitting at the far end of this couch?"

"Because, in my professional capacity, I'm a little leery of you right now. I spoke with Andre this afternoon. He told me you came to see him last night. What're you up to, Josh?"

"Nothing . . . much. Look, Phillip, I had to see him anyway! I promised to get back to him about my visit with Courtney. I was going to tell you about it! I just wanted to test out Ruth's theory."

"What? About Andre being in love with Courtney?"

"Yes . . . and I think she was right on the money. Not that it really means anything."

"Hell, you're right about that! So far, nothing in this case means a damn thing and it's driving me crazy," he said, leaping off the sofa and beginning to pace the floor. Angus sprang off a floor cushion and ran up to the sleeping loft in the next room, his acquired Pavlovian response to Phillip's agitated roaming habits. Jocelyn repressed a desire to follow her cat and asked, "Did you get that lab report you were waiting for?"

She struck a nerve.

"Oho, you bet I did! The last item in a day filled with seemingly unrelated information. I find out from Allen that Jason had put money into *Hedda*—a show he panned *twice!* How do those two facts connect?"

Jocelyn spilled half of her coffee on her lap and didn't even feel the heat. "Saylin was backing *Hedda?* But that's incred——"

"Only in a rational universe. We've clearly stepped through the looking glass with this one. Then I find out that a drug runner, who was killed the night the show opened, was scheduled to make a drop at Saylin's place that same evening. Andre admitted that Jason was expecting a delivery which never came. But there isn't the faintest tie-in between the two deaths. And now *this!*"

"What's *this?* The lab report?"

"Unh-unh . . . the pièce de résistance! The lab boys have determined—beyond a shadow of a doubt—that the strychnine that killed Jason Saylin did *not* come from the rodenticide on the terrace. What was in that vial of cocaine was pure, unadulterated strychnine. No extra additives! A nice *organic* poison."

"You mean somebody *brought* the stuff?!"

"It sure as hell looks that way . . . which blows my spur-of-the-moment theory clear out of the water. This thing was thought out way in advance by someone who knew all the angles—knew that Jason was an epileptic, knew that strychnine causes convulsions similar to a seizure. If I hadn't asked the M.E. to assay the tissues, it would've been a perfect murder!"

"No, no, that can't be right," Jocelyn said numbly, ineffectually dabbing at the coffee stain on her slacks and knowing she sounded inane. Phillip's news had just turned her world upside down and she was searching desperately for a way to right it again. The most upsetting part was her sudden realization that, somewhere in the far recesses of her mind, she had actually accepted the slim possibility that Irene might have killed Saylin—killed him in a moment of blind rage by simply stepping out onto the terrace and reaching into the right sack. Juries understand a "crime of passion," and any decent lawyer could make them understand the kind of passion that takes hold of a brilliant actress whose career has been cruelly thwarted. But what Phillip was describing, no jury in the world could sympathize with, as she herself couldn't. It was too cold and horrifying.

Dumbly, she rose from the couch and went over to the sink,

ostensibly to wet a sponge. Watching her closely, Phillip saw that she was running more cold water over her wrists than the sponge and had a good hunch what was going through her mind. It pained him to see her this way again—up against a wall and scrambling to find a way over—but the hard fact of it was that Jocelyn did her best thinking up against a wall and the pure cop part of him wanted to hear what she came up with.

He didn't have to wait long.

The sponge dropped into the sink with a soggy thud as she whirled around to face him. *"No!* It doesn't make sense, Phillip. There are still too many 'ifs.' For instance, *if* that drug runner hadn't been hit that night, Jason would've gotten his delivery as expected. He would never have opened that second vial, just refilled the first one. How could anybody figure on *that?!"*

"That's a point," he said, sinking down into the rocking chair to mull it over. "Unless . . ."

"Unless what?"

"Unless I've been wrong in thinking there was no connection between the two deaths . . . Unless our killer is even more premeditating than I thought."

From his perch in the bedroom loft Angus watched two silent people, one rocking in a chair and the other running a tap.

CHAPTER XV

"Hey, lady, can you get our ball?"

Jocelyn stuck her foot out to halt the wayward progress of a wet basketball and turned toward the two grinning adolescents who had been practicing lay-up shots on a sodden court in Central Park. The deceptively warm and sunny February morning had obviously seduced them away from their scholastic pursuits. Given the glorious spring-like day and their air of unregenerate jubilance, only a die-hard curmudgeon would have had the heart to scold them.

"Why aren't you guys in school, huh?" Jocelyn scolded, holding the ball aloft in one hand.

"Aw, c'mon, lady," the taller of the two boys said, opening his palms in an appealing gesture, "weren't you ever a kid?"

"Never—I gave it up for Lent." Seeing their faces cloud with bewilderment, she relented. "Oh, what the heck . . . Who am I to judge?"

She hooked the ball up into the air in an easy arc which covered the court and sailed neatly through the hoop. It should have made her day but it didn't, and the accompanying cheers and whistles of the two youths only made her feel worse. She didn't deserve it, she told herself, seeing as how she was embarked on a far more errant venture than a simple day of hookey.

Phillip hadn't spent the night with Jocelyn—hadn't, in fact, been sleeping over since the beginning of the Saylin case. They seemed to have come to a mutual and tacit agreement that sex was not to be used to obliterate the rough edges that needed to be smoothed out between them. Making love, for them, could never be a kind of escape, only a means of discovery.

Still there had been a moment, as Phillip was putting on his coat, when Jocelyn had wanted so badly to bury herself in his arms and to tell him about her date with Marc, in hopes of gaining his understanding, permission . . . whatever. It made no difference. She had already committed to her plan of action, dubious as it was. In no way did she have the right to comfort herself at the expense of his professional ethics. Besides, she reminded herself, he would've said no.

Resolved but still disgruntled, she came out of the Park onto Fifth Avenue and started making her way up the long flight of steps to the Metropolitan Museum. Marc was waiting for her at the top of the stairs, wearing a navy blue wool jacket with matching scarf and darkly tinted Foster Grants, looking like he'd just stepped out of a Modesty Blaise cartoon. She was ready for him.

"Well, if it isn't Agent Double-O Zip! You can relax, Marc. The KGB didn't trail me here."

"Oh, Josh. Thanks for coming. I'm sorry to put you through all this, really."

"Save it. You're not putting me through anything until I get a cup of coffee. Then you can spill your guts until the cows come home . . . and you'd better."

Once inside, they made for the museum cafeteria. Jocelyn secured a table by the reflecting pool while Marc went to fetch coffee and Danishes. As Marc made his way over to their table, Jocelyn observed what looked like a choreographed swiveling of heads as a half-dozen well-groomed ladies followed his progress with avid interest. Personally she had never much fancied the blond, strapping type and it was a keen reminder of how very attractive most women found Marc Carson.

"Josh . . . what're you looking at?"

"Just a room 'breathless with adoration,'" she said smiling to herself, "though not in quite the same sense Wordsworth intended."

Marc wasn't big on classic poetry, but he caught the gist of it and had the good taste to actually blush. This was his saving grace as far as Jocelyn was concerned. Marc was duly aware of his good looks but always a little embarrassed by the impact they made. Being a male model had made him financially secure but acutely uncomfortable. Becoming a lighting designer, with Irene's help and encouragement, had justified his existence and allowed him to feel like more than just a pretty face. Recalling all this, Jocelyn felt herself softening toward him but swiftly squelched the impulse.

"So, what happened last night? Did Irene ever show up at the theatre?"

"God, yes, just barely," he said, rubbing his tired eyes with both hands. "She walked in at ten to eight. They had to hold the curtain fifteen minutes and the understudy had hysterics."

"She was bound to, one way or the other," she said not unkindly, knowing from bitter experience the kinds of misfortune that can befall a star's understudy. "Where had Irene been?"

When Marc balked at answering, she rephrased her question in a blunter mode. "Was she looped?"

Carson shook his head sadly. "Nope, sober as a judge, goddamn it!"

"Well, to quote Donna Reed, 'You're a funny one!' Since when is Irene's sobriety a cause for cursing?"

"Aw, hell, Josh! You know Irene—only two things take her mind off her troubles. One of them's drinking and the other's . . . bed. She won't say a thing about it, so I've been trying to figure which of her old boyfriends she hooked up with—the bitch!"

"I get it—the old tit-for-tat ploy, huh?"

"Yeah, but I didn't *tat!* Not with Courtney . . . not ever."

"Not ever? You sure about that, Marc? Look, I'm not going to blow the whistle on you or anything. After all, you and Courtney go way back and she's a very attractive lady."

"No, no, I swear we never had anything going. Sure, I thought about it once or twice back when we were both modeling—I made a few sly suggestions. But Court wasn't havin' any. She's not like Irene . . . With her, sex is an investment, not a gift. I wasn't going anywhere in those days so there was no way she was going to slip me into her stock portfolio . . . if you see what I mean."

"Perfectly. E. F. Hutton couldn't have said it better. And it makes sense from what I know of Ms. Mason. Did you tell Irene this?"

"I tried but she wouldn't listen. She just threw a fit. I know how she feels, Josh. She's jealous and paranoid . . . and scared. Hell, so am I! I just thought that it would look worse if I *didn't* go see

Courtney . . . as if I had something to hide! But Irene kept ranting, 'Why you, why does she want to see *you?*' "

"Which brings me to my next question. Why you? What did Courtney want to talk to you about, Marc?"

"Well . . . that's the funny thing, see." His voice held a note of trepidation and his hands became very busy with picking slivers of almonds off the untouched pastry in front of him. Jocelyn, on the other hand, took a huge bite out of her Danish and said, "Just give it a shot . . . I love a good yuk with breakfast."

Vehemently flicking a piece of almond into the reflecting pool, he glared at her across the tiny table. "Sometimes you're a real snot, Jocelyn."

"Oh, sticks and stones, sticks and stones," she chanted breezily before leveling him in her best Barbara Stanwyck manner. "Listen, mister, this little tête-à-tête was *your* crappy idea! Don't jerk me around by playing the coy boy or this little snot's going to turn into a great big fink before your very eyes! Now—what happened with Courtney?"

Aware that they were starting to attract more attention than the Vatican exhibit, Carson quickly capitulated. "Okay, Josh, okay . . . I'm sorry. But this is tough. It's gonna sound crazy, especially after what I've been telling you."

"That's alright. I'm infinitely credulous," she cooed in a total about-face.

"Then here goes. We were supposed to have lunch. I went over to the East Side to pick up Court. Patsy wasn't there, and as soon as I got in the door Courtney shoved a glass of wine in my hand and dragged me over to the sofa. She was obviously a couple of drinks ahead of me and pretty keyed up. She started going on about how hard it was to be without Jason—how all alone she felt. She wanted me to know that, no matter what had happened between Irene and Jason, she'd always thought of me as a good friend. That kind of junk."

"But what did she *want*, Marc?"

"A good screw."

A piece of pastry nearly made its way down Jocelyn's windpipe. "She *said* that?!"

"No—she didn't say *that!* She kept talking in her subtle Southern way about 'needing comfort.' But that's what she wanted and no mistake. Christ, I felt like a virgin at a drive-in. I know grief hits some women strangely, but this took the three-tiered cake!"

"What did you do?"

"The only decent thing I could do. When I wasn't playing goalie with my fly, I kept telling her how sorry I was for her and filling her glass. Finally she passed out and I carried her into the bedroom and tucked her in, then left. And that's the truth, Josh."

He downed the remains of his tepid coffee without taking his eyes off Jocelyn's face, waiting for her reaction. Pensively licking crumbs from her fingertips, she met his gaze and said, "It must be. You'd be insane to invent it."

"Well, thank you for that," he sighed, "but what's it going to sound like to Gerrard . . . and how am I going to convince Irene?"

"Convince Irene of *what*, children?"

Jocelyn didn't need to look over her shoulder to see who was behind her. She'd know that voice anywhere, and Marc's apoplexed gaze was all the confirmation she needed. Instead she glanced over toward the cafeteria line to make sure that pasta wasn't on the menu before turning to face her old friend.

"Hello, Irene," she said pleasantly. "You're up early."

"You have to be to catch the *worms*. Isn't that right, Marc?"

"Irene, watch yourself now," he cautioned, casting a worried glance around the room, which had become uncomfortably still.

"Why should I?" she snapped. "I'm sure the police are doing that for me. But don't take my word for it. Ask O'Roarke, here. She's the one with the hotline to New York's Finest . . . which I bet she keeps busy night and day."

Knowing that any attempt at appeasement would only be grist for the Ingersoll mill, Jocelyn took a slow sip of her coffee with feigned calmness and said, "You know, Irenie, you're still a bit too young to play Martha in *Virginia Woolf*, but it's a dandy audition all the same. Whenever you're ready to stop acting, I'd be glad to tell you why I'm here."

Jocelyn had always thought the phrase "piercing glance" to be silly, literary hyperbole, but the look the other woman gave her was nothing short of visual acupuncture.

"I don't need you to tell me a friggin' thing, Beatrice Arnold! There's nothing like a little homicide case to teach you who your friends are—or *aren't*. But I never thought you'd go this far—trying to turn Marc against me, too!"

While Marc was making ineffectual efforts to seat Irene in the chair next to him, Jocelyn rose from hers. She'd gotten all she was going to get out of Marc, who had momentarily lost all powers of speech, and there was no hope of patching things up with Irene, much less getting her to listen to reason. Still, the child-like part of her rebelled at the gross unfairness of her predicament, and she was unable to tear herself away without making a final stab at setting things to right. Like all other instances in her life when she had behaved quixotically, it was a mistake.

"Listen, you pig-headed diva, Marc *asked* me to meet him— because he's concerned in all this because of *you!* I came out of concern for you and because a man was killed. Does that register at all in your self-obsessed little brain? The only way I can help you is to do whatever I can to find out who really murdered Saylin. If that strikes you as an act of betrayal, all I can say is you've been playing scenes too long. This isn't a script. It's real! When a man dies, nobody gets to exit into the wings."

For a flickering instant Jocelyn thought she might be getting through, but there was something in Irene that was congenitally incapable of underplaying a climax. Standing alongside the reflecting pool, she drew herself up to her full statuesque height and arched a superbly scornful brow.

"Me, *pig*-headed? Isn't that the piss pot calling the kettle black, darling? That was an inspired little tirade, though. Did Gerrard give you some special coaching? Obviously, it's not just the *arm* of the law that's very *long*."

"You can go to hell, Irene," she said, seized with an impulse that was as unbelievable to her as it was irresistible, "but before you do, cool off."

In one quick move Jocelyn stiff-armed her open palm into Irene's midriff, catching the taller woman off guard and off balance and sending all five foot ten inches of her backward into the artificial pond. Waves of excited voices lapped around the room, echoing the sound of the water as Jocelyn made a swift about-face and headed out of the building.

She paused halfway down the long stone steps leading to Fifth Avenue, waiting for remorse and shame to overwhelm her. It didn't happen. Instead she felt gloriously cleansed and relieved . . . which was perplexing, considering how she'd wept through all three and a half hours of *Gandhi* the week before. This indecent euphoria lasted until she reached the bottom of the stairs and saw the squad car parked along the curb.

Realizing that very soon the cat would be out of the museum and out of the bag, she made her way back through the park with a heavy heart. The two boys were still playing basketball and cheerfully beckoned her to try her hand at another long shot. The younger boy shot the ball to her, which she dribbled listlessly for a moment before tossing it back, saying, "Sorry, fellas. I'd like to join you but I think I'm about to be called to the principal's office."

CHAPTER XVI

While Irene Ingersoll was receiving her impromptu baptism at the Metropolitan Museum, Phillip Gerrard was driving back to his office from Jason Saylin's funeral service. Last rites for murder victims are always especially grim occasions and Phillip disliked attending them intensely, but he usually went. For one thing he often found them enlightening; the somber formality of the setting demanded a certain reserved decorum from the mourners which was, often times, totally at odds with their true feelings. Everyone feels the strain and, while being in no sense a sadistic cop, he well knew that you could learn a lot from people while they were under stress.

"I thought there would be a bigger turn out, didn't you?" Jerry Fallon asked, breaking in on Phillip's musings. Ever the eager beaver, Fallon had asked to accompany him as soon as he found out that Zito, who was on a surveillance detail, wouldn't be coming.

"No, not really. There'll be a memorial service for Jason later this week at the St. James Theatre. That's when the professional community will turn out."

"A memorial at a Broadway *theatre?!* Geez, that's a little weird, I'd say. But I guess that's show folk for you."

Gerrard's grip on the steering wheel tightened, but he kept his voice bland. "Yes, it is . . . and they'll do a better job of it than what we just sat through."

"You think so?" Fallon asked, taken aback by his superior's unorthodox opinion. Fallon was still of an age where he believed that people of like backgrounds and like education necessarily thought alike. Gerrard was delighted to disabuse him of the idea.

"I *know* so. A while ago my friend Miss O'Roarke took me to the memorial for Harold Clurman at the Shubert Theatre. It was quite something. People who had known and worked with him got up and told wonderful stories, some of them hilarious. It was very moving. You see, I'd never been to a memorial where they spent more time rejoicing in a man's life than bemoaning his departure. The theatre knows how to remember its own—better than most of us."

"Do you think it will be like that at Saylin's?" Jerry asked, somewhat subdued.

After considering a moment, Phillip said, "No, I doubt it. Clurman was universally loved, even as a critic. Jason was feared . . . but respected. Even at his most abusive, he wrote better and more incisively about the stage than anyone else. That's why people like Joc—— Miss O'Roarke got so frustrated with him when he went off on one of his nasty tangents. He wasted his gifts but he got a lot of attention doing it."

Aware that he was out of his depths, Fallon lapsed into silence, leaving Phillip free to continue his speculations. The funeral, even by normal standards, had been a very quiet affair. Courtney Mason had arrived with Patsy Snell in tow. Looking like a *Vogue* layout for deep mourning in a broad-brimmed black hat, Courtney had passed close enough to him in the foyer for Phillip to see that her skin was chalk white under the light dusting of freckles and powder.

Guérisseur had arrived before either of them and was already seated in the front row, looking as damp and stony as a garden gnome after a morning rain. His eyes had been glued on Courtney from the moment she'd entered the parlor, but she had taken a seat at the opposite end of the first row without so much as exchanging a word or a nod with Andre.

The service had been mercifully brief and simple. It wasn't until the minister had mumbled something to Courtney outside the parlor about her "great and senseless loss" that something snapped, and she stumbled toward the waiting limousine with a gloved hand pressed to her mouth, stifling a sob or something worse, with tears streaming down her face.

With surprising quickness Andre had darted out of the building after her and managed to reach the car in time to hold the door open for her and Patsy. Phillip had expected him to join the two women for the ride out to the cemetery—in fact, he saw Andre start to come around to the inside of the car door. But at the last minute Courtney had poked her head out and said something to the hunched little man before snapping the door shut in his face. The limousine had pulled away from the curb swiftly, leaving Guérisseur standing there, head bowed, hands hanging limply at his sides, the epitome of sorrow and rejection. Phillip had started to approach him, but someone had come to take Andre's arm and guide him into another car before Phillip got there. He doubted that Andre had even seen him. The brief glimpse he'd gotten of his face told Phillip that his gaze was directed totally inward.

Pulling into his parking space behind the precinct house, he was now ready to admit that what Jocelyn had dubbed the Ruth Bernstein theory was more than a vague likelihood—a lot more. But whether that constituted a motive for murder was still doubtful. But then, all his possible suspects were a little thin on motive as far as he could see, and this bothered him greatly. He still had no clear idea *why* Jason Saylin had been killed.

Eighty percent of all homicides are spontaneous acts, committed in the heat of the moment. That might have been the case with Saylin's death had the poison come from the terrace greenhouse, but the lab report on the strychnine had put an end to that notion. Someone had gone to a lot of trouble. Strychnine wasn't easy to come by these days. A killer who goes to such lengths usually does so for only one reason—gain. And, for the life of him, Phillip couldn't see who had all *that* much to gain from Jason's death. Irene's success in *Hedda Gabler* wasn't *solely* dependent on Saylin's review; both she and Carson were savvy enough about their profession to know that. Franklin Allen had no apparent reason to do away with a secret investor and potential ally. And Andre had even less reason to suppose that eliminating Jason would secure his heart's desire.

There was, of course, the matter of Courtney Mason, her mysterious pregnancy and the possibility of her inheriting a large part of Saylin's estate. But that made even less sense, considering that abortions are still easily obtainable and that Jason had yet to come to the peak of his earning power as a writer. Whatever her attachment to the man who had impregnated her, her distress over losing Jason seemed genuine enough. And she certainly wasn't the kind of woman to kill a goose while it was still laying golden eggs.

Jerry Fallon coughed a delicate, artificial cough designed to bring his superior's attention to the fact that he had parked the car and been staring blindly at a crack in the windshield for some minutes now. Gerrard grunted and got out of the car, knowing that by evening time tales of his eccentricity would be circulating all over the squad room. Fallon had a mouth almost as big as his ambitions.

Halfway across the parking lot Phillip saw Tommy Zito come out of the back of the building and start hailing him. He sprinted across the graveled lot, ending up directly in front of Gerrard. He looked very red in the face, but not from his brief exertion, Phillip knew. During his days on the beat Zito had run down more hit-and-grab muggers than you could shake a walking stick at; despite being a bit short of leg, Tommy was very long on wind. Something else had knocked the breath out of his right-arm man.

"Fungo, Phil, I'm glad you're here," he said, too excited to even spare a scowl for Fallon. "I didn't know what I was gonna do."

"Do about what?"

"About Miss Ingersoll. She's here with Carson."

"Here?! Cripes, Tommy, you were supposed to tail her, not bring her in."

"I *didn't*. Well, I did, really. But she *made* me . . . walked right up to the patrol car madder than a wet hen, which she was."

"Was what?"

"Wet. We had to mop out the back of the car."

"Okay, okay, take it easy. Now, why is she wet and why did she choose to come here to dry off?"

"She got dunked in the pool at the Metropolitan Museum."

"Slipped?"

Zito shook his head vigorously and said, "Pushed. And now she wants to prefer charges."

Both Tommy's agitation and the scene he was describing struck Phillip's miscreant funny bone, but he kept his features immobile so that Fallon wouldn't pronounce him daft as well as strange to his cohorts.

"Alright, I think I'm with you now. So what charges does she want to make and against whom?"

For the first time Zito became aware of Fallon's presence and made an effort to collect himself. "Well, it's still not settled. Carson's trying to talk her out of it. He's sayin' it was her own fault.

Seems he was havin' breakfast in the cafeteria with . . . someone and she barged in and started sayin' some rotten things."

"So who pushed her, Carson or his friend?"

"His . . . uh . . . friend. And, Phil, now she wants to make it assault and battery!"

"Sure she does. So who's the felon?"

Tommy's color deepened. He watched his left foot make elaborate patterns in the gravel before saying in the smallest of voices, "Josh."

"*Who?!*"

"Uh . . . Miss O'Roarke. She dunked her. Even Carson admits it, but he won't exactly say why."

Jerry Fallon made a strangled sound in his throat that might have become a guffaw if Gerrard's icy gaze hadn't frozen his vocal chords. With a curt nod he strode off ahead of his two subordinates saying, "Okay, let's cut to the heart of this crap. Tommy, you head up to Eighty-fifth Street. Bring her in."

"But, Phil, hey. We don't know—"

"No, but we're going to," he said, stopping to turn ominously toward the other men. "We're all going to know *all* about it. Aren't we, Fallon?"

The younger man's eyes widened in surprise. "Yes, sir. I mean, no sir. I mean—"

"Skip it, Fallon, just skip it."

CHAPTER XVII

True to Murphy's law, all the radiators in the precinct house, which had been performing fecklessly all winter, decided to resume maximum efficiency on the warmest February day since 1956. After ninety minutes of playing Divorce Court with Irene Ingersoll and Marc Carson, Gerrard ran a damp hand through his sweat-matted scalp and picked up the receiver to buzz Zito at his desk.

"You can bring her in now, Tommy."

"Uh . . . you mean Jocelyn?" The static on the intercom made his voice sound doubly doubtful.

"No—I mean Margaret Thatcher! Get her in here, Tom!"

"Well, see, I can't right now. She's not here."

"You let her *leave?!*" He jerked straight up in his chair, his shirt making an adhesive sound coming away from the sticky Naugahyde chair.

"No, hell, no, I wouldn't do that. No, she's just down the hall talking to Marlena."

"Marlena? You mean Harry Grover, the transvestite who wants to be Dietrich?"

"Yeah, Marlena . . . got mugged today at Port Authority. Came in here all hysterical. Geez, his makeup was a *mess!* I was afraid we were gonna have to call Bellevue. But Josh calmed him down . . . took him into the ladies' room and did his face real nice. They're in the ward room havin' coffee and talkin' about *Witness for the Prosecution.*"

"I see. Well, would you tell Miss O'Roarke that unless she's aiming to *become* one, I'd like to see her in here within the next two minutes, please . . . Got that?"

The intercom clicked off immediately and a brief moment later Jocelyn was being ushered through the door by Tommy Zito's right hand and wrist. He was busy using his left arm to keep Harry

Grover from following her into Gerrard's office. Phillip spied a flounce of organdy skirt and heard Harry's smoky contralto.

"And what about *Blonde Venus*—one of her *best!*"

"Yeah, the number in the monkey suit was pretty outrageous," Jocelyn called over her shoulder. "Take care now, Harry. You go look up my friend at the Estee Lauder counter at Saks. She knows *all* about pores."

Before Harry could answer, the door snapped shut behind Jocelyn. She took two small steps into the room in such a typically Jocelyn-like way that Phillip couldn't help but be fascinated by watching her, despite all the harsh words that were on the tip of his tongue. As soon as the door had closed and she knew they were alone together, a deep flush had risen to her face; but she held her head high so that her eyes could scour every nook and cranny of his office. She'd never been here before, and her innate curiosity about people and their environs demanded satisfaction. After pausing a moment to study a Magritte print, the only personal touch in an otherwise austere setting, she brought her gaze up to meet his, her eyes both anxious and amused.

"Don't know about you but I find all this pretty damned uncomfortable. I realize this is all very . . . official but . . . uh . . . *Cosmo* never covered this in any of their dating quizzes. I'm not sure how to act."

"You could start by not acting," he snapped. "That might be helpful."

His tone of voice made her flinch. She'd heard it before, a long while ago, when their relationship was purely businesslike and, oh, so cool. But since then she'd become accustomed to warmer sounds. This sudden reversal, no matter how well deserved, took the heart out of her and left only a cold, stoic misery and a tiny flame of ire.

"I'll spare you the histrionics. Is Irene going to bring charges against me?"

"No. Carson talked her out of it. Said they didn't need that kind of press just now."

"Just Carson talked her out of it?" she asked, trying to keep the faint tremors of hope out of her voice.

"That's right, just Carson." He nodded curtly. "She had a legiti-
mate complaint. It wasn't my place to interfere."

"No, of course it wasn't," she said dully, wandering aimlessly
around the over-heated room while unbuttoning her bulky cardigan. Underneath she wore a gently worn, suede skirt with a bronze-
colored leotard top. Tommy must've caught her in the middle of
her yoga exercises, he thought, trying to shake the memory of all
those fondly observed bending and stretching motions out of his
head. He knew what "the sleep of reason" made and he was struggling hard to keep his wide awake.

"They wouldn't say exactly what led up to your . . . the attack.
I couldn't press them about that once they agreed to let the matter
drop. But I *did* make Carson tell me why you were meeting him
there in the first place. Care to expand on *that?*"

"That depends," she said, leaning against the wall between the
filing cabinet and the door, with an unspoken question in her eyes.
"There are no formal charges against me, right? So, do you want to
talk about the rest of this here . . . or somewhere else?"

"I want to talk about it right here and right now," he said flatly.
"I'm trying to find a killer. I don't have time to fart around while
you play Wonder Woman. That straight enough for you?"

"As an arrow," she said, jerking away from the wall and coming
to face him across the gray metal desk. "And in a minute, I'm going
to tell you where you can stick it! But before I do, I'll give you a
little dirt about my brunch with Marc. Courtney slapped the make
on him when he went to see her yesterday. Bet he didn't mention
that, huh? I got that out of him in five minutes. Down here it
would've taken five hours, and later he'd plead harassment! What
occurs to me is that it's still early days in her pregnancy and she
wants to nail down a possible poppa fast, in case too many people
know about Jason's sterility. That means she's worried about anyone finding out who the real father is. Find him and you'll find
another real hot suspect."

"Brilliant," he said, slapping his hand against the Naugahyde,
sending the chair spinning on its creaking axis. "Your friend tells
you a story and you make this great intuitive leap. How do you
know he wasn't lying? Maybe Courtney's pass had already been
completed previously?. But that's not the *point*, Josh. The point is

you're taking advantage of . . . things. You're interfering here and you have *no* right!"

"Gee, that's funny," she said without a ghost of a smile. "Two days ago I was helping you out—now I'm interfering. You'd better give me a copy of the rules 'cause I'm a bit confused here."

"No, you're not. You're just being stubborn," he said heatedly, then paused a moment to prevent his temper from getting the upper hand. He had forgotten how maddening Jocelyn could be when she put her mind to it. "But, if you want the rules, I'll give them to you. When you give the police pertinent information about a suspect, you're helping. When you take things into your own hands by playing Forty Questions with someone like Carson, not only are you no help, you're a damn menace! This is *not* your affair!"

"The hell it isn't!" She had been on the brink of backing down; in the face of his deadly seriousness, she had even been toying with the idea of apologizing. But his last remark, delivered with a faint hint of Detective Knows Best, had pushed her over the edge. "I *know* these people—I know *you!* You can't just turn me on like a human 'fink' faucet and then shut me off. I have a stake in this, too. I *have* to know who killed Saylin as much as you do!"

"No Josh, you *want* to know. You're trying to satisfy your curiosity. I'm trying to satisfy the law. In order to do that I have to be in an unassailable position. Right now you're jeopardizing that position and I can't risk that."

He sank back into his chair, all his anger ebbing away as swiftly as it had come. Now that the words were out, they both knew that there was more at stake at this moment than an investigation. Jocelyn gazed at him dumbstruck, her eyes bright and glistening, but he knew she wouldn't cry; she was too proud and too hurt for tears.

Softly, with a tiny shake of her head, she said, "You mistake me, sir."

"Maybe I do . . . I don't know. I just know that I have . . ."

"A job to do, I know," she finished for him, clumsily buttoning her cardigan. "And I have no part in it. I know that, too. If that's how it's got to be for you . . . I'll stay out of your way."

Gingerly, like an old person with brittle bones, she slipped the strap of her shoulder bag over her shoulder and started for the door. Gerrard, on a purely involuntary impulse, shot out of his chair, crossed the room in two long strides and spun her around to face him.

"But I don't want you out of my way, Josh."

Her eyes looked past him around the spare and functional office, lingering a moment on the Magritte print of a dark street beneath a sunny sky, while a sad smile crossed her face.

"Yeah, you do, Phillip," she said mildly. "Don't worry about it. You'll be alright. We both will. We've got our work, don't we?"

Gently she extracted herself from his hold and turned to open the door. Halfway through it she paused and looked back at him. "Remember what Carlyle said? 'Blessed is he who has found his work; let him ask no other blessedness.' "

CHAPTER XVIII

"Despite its common usage in the English language, I don't think I've ever, in all my years of vast and varied experience, actually *seen* someone cry into their beer . . . before now," Frederick Revere observed mildly, seated across from a soggy Jocelyn in the barroom of the Players Club. "I think you'd better have another. That one's going to be too salty to finish."

With the barest nod of his silver-maned head he signaled the bartender to bring another round to their table, while Jocelyn attempted to salvage her face with a cocktail napkin.

"Oh lord, I'm sorry, Freddie," she sniffed, dabbing ineffectually but with firm determination. "I didn't mean to get all messy. I hope they don't rescind the new rule about letting ladies into the bar because of this."

"Nonsense—it's the most excitement we've had down here in ages, my dear. Old Phelps just lost his first billiard game in six months because he was so engrossed in our little scene here. Hopefully, he'll start a rumor that I've toyed with your affections and destroyed your young life. Then, maybe, I'll start getting some respect around this place."

Her old friend's wry flippancy succeeded in getting a smile out of Jocelyn. A transplanted Britisher who, in a long and successful career, had garnered both celebrity and the deep admiration of his fellow actors, Revere was a jewel set in the crown of the Players Club, where deference had long since developed into barely concealed adoration. Jocelyn herself had adored him from the first time she saw him onstage. She was still, despite a long acquaintanceship, amazed and grateful that her devotion was returned. Like all the best things in her life, it had come to her freely, without effort. In their first meeting they had discovered a mutual love of Shakespeare, which was Revere's forte, and limericks, which were

Jocelyn's. Challenged to come up with a nasty rhyme about *Titus Andronicus,* Jocelyn had unthinkingly spouted, "Lavinia, daughter of Titus/Has a bark as bad as her bite is/From the forest she's flung/Sans two hands and a tongue/Still she'll write in the sand just to spite us!" Revere had riposted with two lines of Pope's— "Men, some to business, some to pleasure take; But every woman is at heart a rake," and an unbreakable bond was formed.

Jocelyn took a sip of her fresh draft and asked, "Now that the worst of it's over . . . how bad was I? Incoherently hysterical or just whining with self-pity?"

"Neither," Revere said, lighting a long, expensive Cuban cigar, which his doctor expressly forbade him. "For an actor, you have a refreshing fear of bathos. You're just very hurt and that's hard on you. I was like that at your age—could tear a passion to tatters on stage but avoided them like the plague in my personal life—until I married Lydia, of course. There's no such thing as aesthetic distance when you love someone, my dear."

"Frederick, I know that! But this isn't just love. It's Phillip's *work* I've been meddling in and it's very serious business . . . but I just can't seem to keep my nose out of it and I can't bear to be excluded."

"That *is* love," he said, taking a complacent puff. "And you can't compartmentalize it because you're not built that way . . . thank God. You don't know how to wait in the wings for your man—just like Brutus's wife in *Julius Caesar.*"

"Oh, God, are you going to quote at me now?"

"Damn right, that's how I earn my keep around here since I retired." He leaned back in his chair and blew out two perfect smoke rings before disclaiming in a velvety crystal voice that still sent shivers up her spine, "Am I yourself/But, as it were, in sort or limitation,/To keep with you at meals, comfort your bed,/And talk to you sometimes? Dwell I but in the suburbs/Of your good pleasure?"

He cut short his recitation as the entire bar fell silent and Jocelyn looked dangerously close to a fresh onslaught of tears. Afraid that she would remember the next two lines of the speech, he sought to divert her.

"Anyway, let's take it as given that you are concerned in this whole affair. Age has taught me discretion, and I'm perfectly willing to play Watson to your Holmes. So, who do you have pegged as Saylin's killer?"

His tactic had the desired effect. Jocelyn bolted up in her chair with a sharp shake of the shoulders and said, "That's just it . . . I can't think of a *soul* who would really want Jason dead! Phil—I mean, the police—focus on things like means, opportunity and motive. Their idea of motive is that a *lot* of people hated Jason's guts . . . which is true. In his time, he'd bad-mouthed about every working actor on Broadway. Saylin left von Stroheim in the dust as far as being the man you love to hate."

"Makes quite an awesome task for the police, doesn't it," Revere mused as a mischievous grin lit up his face. "Too bad they can't hold open calls for suspects. I know some actors who'll audition for *anything.*"

It was a small joke, but it was enough for Jocelyn, who threw back her head and crowed. She hadn't had a good laugh in days and Frederick's levity was just the tonic she needed. Seeing the sparkle return to her eyes, he took a long, satisfied draw on his cigar and waited for her to collect herself.

"God, that's good. That's exactly how absurd it is, you see. I just can't feature Jason's death as some grotesque recreation of *Murder on the Orient Express* with a cast, literally, of thousands, each one bearing a tiny grain of strychnine up to his penthouse!"

Jocelyn paused to take a ruminative sip of ale, then continued more seriously. "It may be that each man kills the thing he loves, but what about the thing he hates? We all know critics are a necessary evil and, God knows, Saylin could be one of the evilest . . . but maybe that's what made him so *necessary.*"

"Yes, I see what you mean. As Mr. Dooley said, 'Life'd not be worth livin' if we didn't keep our inimies.' But, Josh dear, if we *do* eliminate all the members of Actors Equity, what does that leave you with?"

"Damn little," she said despondently. "A fiancée who was nuts about the man, and his oldest friend who's nuts about the fiancée. And therein lies a tale."

Over a third round of drinks Jocelyn filled Revere in on the curious saga of Jason, Courtney and Andre. Somewhere in the middle of her narrative he let his cigar go out and forgot to relight it. When she'd finished, he was leaning forward, both elbows propped up on the table, allowing his hands to support a slack jaw.

"Ye gods and little fishes! It's like something out of Victor Hugo. Does Andre know about Miss Mason's pregnancy?"

"Oh, no. Out of the question! She'd be furious if she knew that Patsy told me, and Andre's the last person she'd want to hear about it . . . which is for the best right now. I don't think the poor man could take much more than he already has."

"I gather then that Guérisseur isn't your prime candidate?"

"Oh, Freddie, I don't know. I can't help feeling sorry for the man because he's obviously in such pain. But how do I know that's not just remorse? Phillip did manage to teach me a thing or two about being objective, and *objectively* he has two strong motives—passion and gain. He will inherit from Jason's estate. Plus, he had the means—he lived with the man and had access to all his belongings."

"Yet, me thinks I hear a 'but' hovering in the air."

"Well . . . yes! Call it professional bias if you like, but I spend twelve hours a week haranguing my students with the notion that action comes out of character . . . which leaves me with the belief that Andre just isn't the right *type*. He's the fastidious, repressed sort. Pushed beyond his limits, he might pull a trigger or swing a club, but *poison* someone? It just doesn't figure."

"You have a point there," he said, elegantly wiping a fleck of foam from his moustache. "Poisoning isn't just insidious, it bespeaks cruelty, the desire to see your victim suffer. I can't imagine that a man who writes with his delicacy—"

"Writes?! How did you know Andre wrote? I mean, what did you read?"

"Well, just skimmed actually. It was a book about forgotten film stars."

"*Lost Ladies*, right! Where on earth did you find a copy of that?"

"Oh, I don't *have* the book. I just picked it up to look at when I was at the Above Boards Theatre a few months ago. Franklin had asked me in to talk about a revival of *Major Barbara*. He was trying to lure me out of retirement to play Undershaft. Might've worked too if he hadn't kept talking about making Shaw 'relevant.' Shaw was *always* relevant, even when he was rotten! Anyway, at some point Franklin was called out of his office to attend to something and I was left twiddling my thumbs for about twenty minutes. The book was on his shelf and I saw Guérisseur's name on the binding, so I just picked it up out of curiosity. What I read was quite good, very affectionate and rather wicked at the same time. Wonderful style. I wonder why he didn't write more."

"I guess that was why he was getting out—there wasn't enough room for two writers in that 'family.' Makes sense knowing what Saylin's ego was like. What did Franklin say about the book?"

"Very little. I think he was irritated with me for filching it off the shelf. He put it right back and then we started arguing about updating Shaw and things came to a pretty hasty close after that."

"Speaking of things coming to a close. I should be heading home, Freddie. I've been bending your ear for nearly three hours. It must be near the breaking point by now."

"Oh, piddle. My joints are a little stiff but my ear's as supple as it ever was, especially when it's bent to your dulcet tones, dear heart."

"Oh, g'arn," Jocelyn said in her best Eliza Doolittle, "H'm jist a poor gel, I am."

"No, you're not but you're a tired one, I can see that. Heaving Irene Ingersoll into a fish pond is no small feat, my child. You need to get some rest so, much as I hate to lose your company, I'll now escort you to the door."

They dickered pleasantly for a few moments over who would pick up the tab until Jocelyn, observing their unstated tradition, admitted defeat. Walking into the warmly lit lobby of the Players Club, she realized how depleted she felt and how reluctant she was to remove herself from Frederick's comforting presence. His gentle air of solicitude as he helped her on with her coat and scarf only made things more difficult. As always, he intuited her mood perfectly and, tucking her scarf around her neck, said, "Don't worry, Josh. You've just hit a bad patch. We all have them. When this whole mess is over, you bring your detective fellow to meet me. I'll give him a few pointers on how to live with a strong-minded female. God knows, I've had the practice."

Reminded of Revere's enduring devotion to the memory of his

late wife and their thirty-year marriage, Jocelyn felt herself starting to choke up again. "Thanks, Freddie . . . but I really don't know if my detective fellow's going to be around anymore. I think I might lack your staying power."

"Nonsense. Remember our favorite sonnet? Will never lies," he said bending over to whisper in her ear. "Let me not to the marriage of true minds/Admit impediments. Love is not love/Which alters when it alteration finds,/Or bends with the remover to remove."

Buoyed up by beer, kind words and rekindled hope, Jocelyn charmed her cab driver into running red lights all the way up to Eighty-fifth Street. Once inside her apartment, she headed straight for her phone machine. But there was no message from Phillip, only a reminder from Ruth Bernstein that she was due to make an appearance at their friend Merle's baby shower the next day.

Dutifully, Jocelyn began gift wrapping her embryo offering as she switched on the television to catch the last half of *Pat and Mike* on the late show. It was her favorite Tracy-Hepburn film, and its charm remained intact for her even after a dozen viewings. But this time, when Spencer told Katharine that he thought they "made a good team," she found herself weeping into a pair of bunny feet.

CHAPTER XIX

"Ruthie, it's Josh. What time is Merle's shower?"

"Cripes, you are hopeless," Ruth Bernstein sighed. She was long accustomed to her friend's sporadic senility but aggrieved at having to cope with it on the phone at nine in the morning, her least sympathetic hour. "You've only known about this shower for two months now! It's for *five.* Remember, Merle said she wanted a cocktail-hour shower so she could see her friends swilling down all the hooch she's been deprived of for seven months?"

"Oh, right. I forgot Merle was into S-and-M pregnancy."

"Cute, very cute. Is this the kind of snideness I can expect when Jake and I decide to procreate?"

"Not at all. I shall be filled with reverential protectiveness. I even plan on hiring several Hell's Angels to escort you to your Lamaze classes."

"I'm touched. What's up? Why are you in such a snit?"

"I'm *not,*" Jocelyn protested feebly, knowing that Ruth's keen ear was already picking up on her subtext. "I just have a bunch of things to do today."

"Yeah? Such as?"

"Well, I have to get another shower gift for Merle for one thing."

"What for? The bunnies die?"

"Sort of . . . Actually they're alive but kind of smudged. No kid should have to begin life with smudged bunnies."

"I know you believe you're making some kind of sense, so I'll chalk this up to acute distraction. What is it, the Saylin thing or trouble with Phillip?"

"Oh, six of one, a half dozen of the other. I'm just having some trouble with my subdivision right now."

"Jocelyn, are you smoking those funny cigarettes at this hour of the morning?" Ruth asked, trying to sound severe while stifling a yawn, "because your lucidity level is very low at this moment."

"I know, I know I sound inane. Just bear with me. Look, if I'm a bit late for the shower, will you make my apologies to Merle and tell her I'll be there as soon as I can?"

Much as she would've liked to unburden herself to her best friend, Jocelyn squelched the impulse for several reasons: a) she didn't have much time; and b) Ruth was, in many ways, much like Phillip in that she put little stock in hunches and frowned on impulsive behavior. Jocelyn could barely justify what she was about to do to herself, so she knew that she didn't stand a ghost of a chance in selling Ruth on the idea. Better to let sleeping dogs lie. Unfortunately, Ruth's canine instincts were swiftly awakening.

"Ahh . . . I don't know. Your voice has gone tricky. I remember you sounding like this when you did *The Little Foxes* two summers ago. What're you up to?"

"Nothing much. Very little, really. I'll tell you all about it later."

It was the wrong thing to say. Curiosity only kills cats; it is the stuff of life to young Jewish matrons.

"Tell me now."

"Can't. There's not enough time. But, if it will make you feel any better, Ruth, I'm just going to see a man about a book. Bye."

On her way down to the Above Boards Theatre, Jocelyn swung by Macy's to pick up a new baby gift and, hopefully, assuage an uneasy conscience. Under pressure she was, as Ruth had said, a decisive shopper. Within fifteen minutes she had spied and purchased a charming three-dimensional crib mobile, hung with ducks and fishes filled with a mysterious colored fluid. If the kid stares at this long enough, he'll never need to take drugs, she thought, fighting her way through the revolving door and back onto the street.

Riding the subway down to Twenty-third Street, she tried to catch her breath and collect her thoughts—tried, in fact, to figure out what exactly she hoped to accomplish on this fool's errand. All she knew was, since Frederick's mention of it the night before, she'd had an irresistible urge to get her hands on a copy of Andre Guérisseur's book. It had nothing to do with what Phillip called "hard proof"—it had nothing to do with proof at all. She just wanted to see what the man had written. Having, like so many actors "between engagements," taken several stabs at writing herself, she was well aware that authors invariably revealed as much about themselves as they did about their themes. If she was reading Guérisseur's character wrong, if there were more potential there for mayhem than she'd seen, hypothetically his book might help set her straight. And his book was in Franklin Allen's office.

This led her to her real problem—what was she going to say to Franklin and how was she going to get her hands on the book? Her gut feeling was that the direct approach would not work. Allen was a subtle director and a subtle man. Whether or not he actually had something to hide, his basic tendencies were never toward laying all his cards on the table. Also, he was nobody's fool, and since he knew about her vested interest in the Saylin case she would need a very plausible excuse for turning up at the theatre—and fast. Twenty-third Street was just one stop away.

Walking into the Above Boards' immaculate but miniscule lobby, she still hadn't formulated a plan. As luck would have it, she ran smack into Allen, who was seated on an oak bench and conferring with his stage manager over coffee and a prompt book. But luck was on her side as Franklin's first words gave her the inspiration for the scene she was about to improvise.

"Well, if it isn't Miss O'Roarke—actress, teacher and wetter of hens! You know, I should be very cross with you, Josh," he remonstrated unconvincingly. "I had a sneezy, sniffling Hedda onstage last night, thanks to you. Philosophically, I abhor violence no matter what the provocation. But, on the practical side, I can't see that it did Irene any harm. She actually paid attention to the notes I gave her afterward, which was refreshing. I may hire you on a steady basis."

"Then you've got a deal, Franklin. But you should know I come here not to dunk Caesar but to *replace* her."

Hardly believing what had just come out of her mouth, Jocelyn felt her heart racing. She studied the reaction of the two men on the bench. Geoff Lewis, Allen's stage manager, went bug-eyed and let his prompt book slide onto the lobby floor. But the unflappable Franklin was still grinning faintly while his eyes bore into hers.

"*Replace* Irene? I don't quite follow, Jocelyn. Irene has a six-month contract and we're doing quite nicely at the box office. Why should I want to replace her, pray tell?"

Steadily returning his gaze, she fished a cigarette out of her bag and lit it with slow deliberation before replying, "Oh, I'm not saying that you *want* to replace her, Franklin, but you may *have* to in the not-too-distant future. Now, I know you'd like to be prepared, as far as possible, for whatever contingencies might arise. I just thought I might be able to help you get a jump on things, if you see what I mean?"

She managed to keep her tone both bantering and ominous, and it had its effect. Allen wasn't rattled, but his interest was definitely piqued. With a great show of nonchalance, he turned to his stage manager.

"Geoff, after you get all those messy papers in order, why don't you go check on the cast. Tell them we'll start "Act Two" in about twenty minutes. I'll be up in my office with Jocelyn until then."

As Lewis scuttled into the house, Jocelyn followed Allen up the stairs to his office. She knew that by the time *Earnest* rehearsal began, word would be out that she was after Irene's job. In theatrical parlance, it would be very "hot dish," as her friendship with Irene was well known and long-standing. Coupled with whatever rumors were circulating about their run-in at the Metropolitan, this news would catapult Irene and Jocelyn into the ranks of major feuding rivals, making Fontaine and DeHavilland look like fond siblings by comparison. The exquisite and painful irony of the situation wasn't lost on Jocelyn, but she was past agonizing about it. In her muddled attempts to help Phillip and protect Irene, she had only succeeded in alienating the affections of both of them. Having utterly failed as an altruist, she was now firmly committed to her own ends—to snoop.

Sauntering into the office behind Allen, she resolutely shut the door and plunked herself down in the chair facing his desk.

"So, Franklin, how's it going with *Earnest?*" she asked casually, reaching for his ashtray. "Billy having fun with Lady Bracknell?"

"Yes, I think so. But you know Billy. He's deeply entrenched in The Method. Yesterday he started getting cramps. Had to take a Midol. Want some coffee?"

Without waiting for a reply, he moved over to the electric percolator on the windowsill and filled two Styrofoam cups, one of which he handed to Jocelyn, who accepted it eagerly.

"Well, I'm not The Method type, myself. Also, I seldom get cramps and never take Midol. So, what do you say?"

"Ah, small talk time's over, is it," Franklin said, seating himself behind his desk. "You're really serious about this then, Josh? What makes you think I'm going to lose Irene?"

"Oh, come on, Frank! What do you expect me to say? A little bird told me? Anyway, it wouldn't be the truth. I don't know a damn thing, anymore than you do. I'm just a good guesser, and my guess is that the police are getting very itchy. They're going to want to make an arrest soon."

"And you're guessing they'll plump for Irene?" he asked, giving her an intimate and cajoling smile.

"Now don't get cunning with me, Franklin. It won't play. I didn't come here to be pumped about the investigation. This is strictly shop business. You don't want to get caught with your pants down and, the way I see it, I'm the best kind of insurance you could have."

The scene was playing out nicely for Jocelyn. Like many a forceful director, Allen had a secret craving to be bullied from time to time, which she was satisfying adeptly. Added to that, her ambivalent air of innuendo and rectitude had worked his curiosity up to a fever pitch. She knew that he would be much more likely to let something slip if he thought that he were the one doing the dredging.

"But why are you my *best* insurance, Jocelyn? I don't mean to sound insulting—I know you're a fine actress—but you're not exactly a 'name,' are you, darling?"

"If I were, would I be sitting here?" she shot back. "Face it, sweetie, if your leading lady gets indicted for murder, the only 'names' you'll be able to find will be in the phone book!"

"Why, Josh," he said, both shocked and delighted, "I've never known you to be so sublimely crass."

"Crass, my ass! I'm just telling you what you already know. So far the publicity from Jason's death hasn't hurt *Hedda*—quite the contrary, I'd guess. This early in the run, you're still getting an 'in' theatre crowd and they don't mind a whiff of scandal. They rather like it. But in a little while your box office is going to need the 'bus and tunnel' houses—the tourists. They get all their gore and violence on TV. When they come to the theatre, they come for a more 'uplifting' experience. If Irene gets pegged for killing Saylin, your Broadway baby's going to develop a sudden sag . . . unless you turn it around."

"How can I?" Allen managed to keep his tone totally neutral, but the enlarged pupils and shallow breathing told her that she had his undivided attention. He was waiting for her next move and she had to make it. She felt her scruples strain like tendons, but it was too late to back off.

"By hiring the arresting officer's girlfriend, that's how. Phillip will make the arrest, you know. Just think of it! I mean, it's sick but it's a P.R. man's dream come true. Justice is done, virtue is rewarded. It could make the front page of the *Post.*"

Propping her feet up on his desk, she downed the last of her coffee and took grim satisfaction in the effect she'd made. Never in her life had she seen a man so torn between terror and titilation.

"But, my God," he said, holding his head with both hands, "it's so utterly . . . grotesque!"

"Yeah . . . and it would sell a *lot* of tickets."

"Christ almighty, that it would," he said, getting up to pour himself another cup of coffee. Too shaken for good manners, he forgot to offer Jocelyn a refill. She saw what would have been her portion splash into a spider plant as he set down the pot with an unsteady hand. "It's beyond Machiavellian by light years! Whatever made you . . . I mean, you're *friends* . . . how can you—"

A knock on the door prevented him from finishing his question, for which Jocelyn, fearing that her improvisational abilities were about to be taxed beyond their limit, gave silent thanks. Geoff Lewis stuck his head in the office and said, "I'm sorry to interrupt, Franklin, but Marc Carson's here and he'd like to see you. He wants to set levels for the tea-party scene."

"Oh, Marc. Yes, of course. Tell him I'll be right down. Thanks, Geoff."

Lewis popped out of the office as quickly as he'd come in and Jocelyn, eager to keep Allen from finishing his question, said, "Marc's doing the lighting for *Earnest?* I didn't know that."

"Oh, yes, yes, naturally," Franklin murmured, gulping half of his still-steaming coffee without a quiver. "I was delighted with his work on *Hedda* . . . delighted. He's very talented. I plan to use him a lot. Look, Jocelyn, could you wait here a bit? I have to check those lights and I need a little time to . . . digest, you understand."

"Completely. I can hang about for a while. But I have an appointment uptown and you have a rehearsal to get on with. If I'm not here when you get back, just call my agent. He's very discreet."

"Ah, yes . . . Knowing you, he must be," Allen said, scurrying toward the door. With his hand on the doorknob he stopped to turn back toward her, his eyes narrowed with sudden suspicion. "Say, Josh, this thing between you and Irene. It doesn't have anything to do with Marc, does it?"

Considering the little bombshell she'd just dropped on him, Jocelyn found this question remarkably superfluous, coming from someone as hard-nosed about business matters as Franklin. More surprising was the look of genuine concern on his face and the slight flinch of his shoulders, as if he were expecting to receive a blow. This sudden flash of real emotion caught her off guard, and she had to check an impulse to reassure him in order to maintain her persona of the total enigma.

"Why . . . would it make a difference, Franklin?" she asked cooly, stretching her arms high above her head as if she were suppressing a yawn.

"No . . . I don't know . . . It might," he floundered, uncertain of his ground.

Taking a nail file out of her bag, Jocelyn began delicately filing her index finger. "Well, I wouldn't worry about it if I were you. Like I said, this is strictly business. My reasons are my reasons and . . . like any gift horse, I don't like having my molars examined. So you just run it up your mental flagpole and see if it makes you feel like pledging allegiance."

"Alright, I'll do that," Allen said with a laugh, trying to regain his old nonchalance. "As long as I don't have to sign in blood."

After the door closed, Jocelyn continued filing until she heard Allen's footsteps recede down the stairs. Then she dropped her file, her bag and her Joan Crawford impersonation and shot over to the bookcase. Franklin's floor-to-ceiling bookcase contained a comprehensive collection of theatre scripts and texts but in no discernible order. It took her ten agonizing minutes to ferret out the copy of *Lost Ladies*, which was on the bottom shelf stuck behind a bulky edition of *European Theories of Drama* at the back of the row.

The very placement of the book excited her curiosity. Frederick had spotted it earlier with a casual glance, which meant that, since Revere was not endowed with X-ray vision, Franklin had seen fit to relocate it to the dimmest recess possible. But, despite the obscurity of its position, the book was not dusty and showed no signs of neglect. Flipping it open to the title page, she found an inscription, "To Ainsly—and a new beginning, From Andre." So this was Jason's own copy! How in the world, she thought, did Franklin get his hands on it?

Filled with hopeful expectance, she made a quick survey of the table of contents and began scanning the first chapter, using the long-dormant skills she'd acquired in a high-school speed-reading course. By the end of the chapter, which dealt mainly with the roots of the star system in Hollywood, she was cursing herself and Evelyn Wood for being fools. It was like a bad day's shopping—when you don't know exactly what you're looking for, there's never enough time.

With one ear cocked to the door and a growing sense of panic, she leafed madly through the pages. Midway through a chapter on Gladys Fenton, a forties' ingenue whose name rang only the tiniest of bells in Jocelyn's head, she spotted something. A long paragraph detailing Gladys's fate after her star had waned had been bracketed in red ink. At the bottom of the paragraph, written in the margin in a minute but concise script, was the notation "Ck. vs. S. rev. for 'F. Flowers', '79."

Intending to copy the passage into her notebook, Jocelyn, sitting cross-legged on the floor, made a long reach toward her bag. Her hand had just grabbed the shoulder strap when she heard a soft padding in the corridor. A moment later Geoff Lewis, who like most stage managers moved on little cat's feet, popped into the office to find Jocelyn lolling in her chair, smoking a cigarette.

"Josh, I'm sorry, but Franklin's going to be tied up for a while.

There's a big hassle going on with the costume designer. Billy's unhappy about his bustle."

"If he's unhappy now, just wait till he sees the corset. I believe the first corset was based on a drawing found in de Sade's notebooks," Jocelyn said, lazily getting up from the chair and hiking her bag over one shoulder. "Anyway, much as I'd like to stay and watch Billy bust his bustle, I've got to mosey."

"Right," Geoff said eagerly, anxious to get back to rehearsal. Politeness, or Franklin, required that he escort her down the stairs to the lobby. If Lewis was any indication, her improvised performance had been a complete success. He practically bowed her out the front door with near oriental courtesy. Considering the fact that they'd done summer stock together eight years ago, it was an object lesson for Jocelyn in how stars got to be stars—they *acted* like one.

She was halfway onto the pavement when Geoff remembered something. "Oh, Jocelyn, Franklin said to tell you that he'd get back to you tonight or tomorrow morning at the very latest."

"Hmm, I'm sure he will." And she was *very* sure, as she set her course eastward, that she'd be hearing from Allen before the day was out. It wouldn't take him very long to discover that he'd lost his *Lost Ladies*.

CHAPTER XX

"Hi, this is Jocelyn speaking to you via the wonders of modern technology. If you hate talking to these damn machines as much as I do, just lean back, shut your eyes and pretend you're speaking to your therapist. I get the *best* messages this way—"

Phillip Gerrard put down the receiver for the third time that morning without waiting for the beep. If Jocelyn had answered the phone, he would've said something—what, he had no idea—but he had absolutely nothing remotely meaningful to relate to a recording. He was rankled on several counts: a) that she wasn't home; b) that she had the cheek to leave a smart-ass message on her machine when, by rights and the logic of a closet romantic, she should have been too distressed to do more than snivel a miserable greeting; and c) that the Saylin case was going nowhere.

The lab boys had, at his insistence, checked and triple-checked the two vials found at Jason's apartment for fingerprints and come up with nothing. Cut crystal was not the kind of surface that prints adhered to, and the silver tops were grooved along the side and had too small a space on their tops to provide identifiable prints.

The possible connection between the drug runner's death and Saylin's, which had looked so promising at first, was petering out fast. According to Jerry Fallon, who was doing his Dick-Tracy damndest, all the signs still pointed to some street thugs who got lucky, and they'd already lined up several likely suspects from their JD files.

But the real thorn in his side, which he'd confided to no one, not even Jocelyn or Tommy, had to do with the night of Saylin's death. No stranger to violence and sudden death, he had been as shocked as the rest of the party when Jason went into his fatal seizure . . . because he hadn't *felt* it coming, and this bothered him. Despite the careful methodology he brought to his work and preached endlessly to his subordinates, he relied, more than he'd realized, on his instincts. Coming to know Jocelyn had made him appreciate the value of such an asset. Her special skill was a nose for people, his was a nose for danger. But despite all the edgy crosscurrents floating around the penthouse that evening, he hadn't picked up a whiff of real menace. It troubled him deeply. Either there was a fluke element to this murder which he hadn't discovered or he was slipping; he devoutly hoped it was the former.

Brooding about things wasn't going to help any, he told himself, as he leaned forward to press the intercom and summon Zito into his office. If his sixth sense was failing him, his best bet was to rely on Jocelyn's.

"What's up, Phil?" Tommy asked, closing the door behind him with uncharacteristic gentleness. Ever since the fight with Jocelyn, Zito had been treating Gerrard with the kind of solicitude usually reserved for cancer-ward patients. Somehow, over the past week, Jocelyn had unknowingly alchemized Tommy's jaundiced opinion of her into one of high regard. His doleful brown eyes spoke volumes of regret for Phillip's having blown a good thing. The fact that Gerrard tacitly agreed with him didn't keep him from wanting to throttle his friend. "Hey, I got that copy of Saylin's last review from Guérisseur if you want to look at it. Boy, it's a real killer—I mean, it's pretty awful."

"No, just bring it along. I'll look at it on the way."

"On the way where?"

"We're going to pay a call on Miss Mason, Thomas. We haven't had a talk with her since the initial questioning. I think we've allowed enough time for her to get over the first shock. Now we're going to lean a little."

"On *her?* Christ, what for? She's totally out of it. What's she gonna be able to tell us?"

"With any luck, who knocked her up."

A grim-faced Patsy Snell ushered Gerrard and Zito into the living room on East Seventy-sixth Street, where Courtney Mason sat on a low sofa fitting pictures into a photo album. Sitting there placidly in a jade-green silk kimono with a dreamy look on her face, Courtney appeared to Phillip not totally out of it but still far from all there. Her face was heavier than he remembered, a trace of

jowliness around the delicate jaw bones. This could be attributed to
the onset of pregnancy, but his guess was that the standard symptoms of cocaine withdrawal had set in; the body metabolism slows
back down, causing weight gain.

"Courtney, ducks, brace yourself," Patsy said, pulling a box of
Sherman Ovals out of her shirt pocket. She lit one and jerked her
head in Gerrard's direction. "You've got gentlemen callers."

A sudden light came into her eyes as she lifted her head with a
welcoming smile. Seeing who her callers were, the light died out
and a tiny crease appeared between her finely tweezed eyebrows,
but the smile stayed in place.

"Why, Mr. Gerrard, how nice. I was just thinkin' of you . . .
how sweet it was of you to come to the funeral and all. But I'm
forgetting my manners. Who's your nice friend there?"

It took Tommy a second or two to realize that she was referring
to him. When he did, he turned beet red and stammered, "I'm
. . . uh . . . we met before, Miss Mason . . . at the theatre.
I'm Thomas Zito."

"Oh, of course! You're Jocelyn's friend. Well, y'all *both* are, naturally. How silly of me. I truly don't know where my head is these
days." She gave Tommy the sweetest of smiles, then added, "You
do forgive me, don't you?"

As Zito was clearly incapable of answering with more than a
dumb nod, Patsy, with her usual efficiency, covered the gaffe by
offering drinks all around. Courtney was the only taker. After handing her a large tumbler of wine and Perrier, the older woman
pleaded work and made her escape into the next room, but not
without shooting Phillip a hard, quizzical glance before she left.

Once Patsy was out of the room, Phillip motioned Tommy into a
chair and pulled an ottoman over to the sofa for himself. Courtney
had become reimmersed in her photo album and, sensing that his
usual direct approach would be fatal just then, he leaned over to
look at the snapshots and asked in a calm, gentle voice, "Where
were these pictures taken, Miss Mason?"

"Oh, pshaw. You don't have to 'Miss' me," she said without
really looking up from the album, a sly grin playing around the
corners of her mouth. "I just called you 'Mr. Gerrard' to be polite

in front of Patsy. But you're an old pal of Jason's, not to mention bein' Joshie's beau. You just call me Courtney."

"Alright . . . Courtney."

"That's better. Anyway, these here are shots of our last vacation. Back in November, we all went down to Mexico—Jason, me and Andre." She paused to hand him a photo and take another pull at her drink, each sip of which seemed to thicken her drawl. "Look it this one. It's one of my very favorites."

Taken against the background of a colorful street bazaar, the picture showed Courtney, in a canary-yellow sundress, standing between a leering Jason Saylin and a slightly abashed looking Guérisseur, both men wearing identical sombreros.

"I bought them those hats in the market that morning and made them wear 'em *all* day long," she giggled. "Ol' Andre was just plain mortified but Jason . . . well, Jason knew how to take a joke. Besides, he could wear anything and make it look good."

He handed the photo back, marveling at the fierce look of possessive pride which suffused Courtney's face as she stared at the shot. Despite Jocelyn's many wry dissertations on the makeup of Southern women, Phillip was still taken aback by the almost palpable aura of tenacity emanating from the fragile figure opposite him. Even death, the ultimate negator, had failed to diminish Courtney's will to hold on.

Striving to sound casual, he asked, "So a good time was had by all then?"

"Oh, Jason and I had a wonderful time, really perfect. I don't know about Andre. One night—I don't mean to be tellin' tales now," she temporized, the glint in her eyes belying her words— "but one night, Andre sneaked off to a, um, the red-light district, see? Next morning, he came back all peaked. Had dysentery something fearful for 'bout three days . . . and serve him right, as my momma'd say."

The grin had spread to the rest of her face as she went back to shuffling through the snapshots. It pointed up the delicate crow's feet around her eyes, but she still had the look of a child enjoying a private joke. Gerrard felt like a surgeon performing the vaguest kind of exploratory operation and not knowing where to poke or probe next. However, his next question hit a nerve.

"Have you spoken to Andre since the funeral?"

Tendrils of red hair flew away from her face as she jerked herself upright. "No. Why should I? . . . Have you?"

The accusatory note in her voice surprised him. "No, not since the funeral. Any reason I should?"

She took another long sip of wine and her tone became more conciliatory. "Well, I 'spect you know how to do your job . . . And, I mean, it must be terribly difficult, him bein' your friend and all, still—" She was cut short by the ringing of the telephone, which sat on the oak end table by the sofa. Courtney made no move to answer it and, after a moment, they could hear Patsy taking the call in the other room. Shortly, Patsy appeared in the archway, a fresh Sherman stuck in the corner of her mouth and a slide rule in an ink-stained hand. "It's for you, Court," she said, her voice brusque but holding a note of wariness. "It's Dr. Aguerra."

Without sparing a glance in her direction, Courtney said flatly, "Tell him I'll call back later."

But Gerrard had other plans. "Oh, no. Don't do that on my account, please," he said gallantly, reaching over to lift the phone from the end table and deposit it in Courtney's lap. "I know how impossible it is to reach doctors during their office hours. You go right ahead."

Confounded, as he knew she would be by his apparent chivalry, she picked up the receiver charily as if it were an explosive device. "Hello, Dr. Aguerra. Yes, it's me. How're things?"

There was no chance of hearing the voice on the other end of the line. Courtney kept the receiver pressed tight against her ear, but the increasing whiteness of her knuckles and the mounting alarm in those enormous green eyes told him that "things" were not hunky-dory. When at last she spoke, her voice was careful and restrained. "Yes, I understand, doctor . . . It's definite then . . . No, I'm not sure about that yet. I'll let you know. Bye now."

In the ensuing silence Courtney drained the contents of her glass and held it out to Patsy for a refill. Whatever doubts he'd had about his instincts, Phillip knew they were dead on the money now. He waited until Patsy had brought the fresh drink and Courtney was about to raise it to her lips before he said quietly, "You know,

Courtney, it's not a good idea to drink so much when you're pregnant."

The hand holding the glass stopped in midair while her eyes flew
from Gerrard's face to Patsy's and then back again. For an instant
she looked like a doe frozen by the glare of oncoming headlights,
but then something shifted behind those eyes and the glass reached
its destination. With an air of defiance she downed half the drink
and then said, "Well, aren't you the clever one, Mr. Phillip? But
then, you'd have to be to keep up with Joshie, wouldn't you? I've
never found her all that endearing, to tell you the truth, but she's a
very popular girl . . . I mean, sooner or later, *everybody* talks to
Joshie. *Don't* they, Patsy, honey?"

Patsy Snell seemed to have aged five years while standing in that
archway. Looking pained and almost fearful, unable to meet the
other woman's caustic gaze, she threw her hands up as if in surren-
der and turned to walk out of the room. Courtney waited for the
sound of the front door closing, then turned back to Gerrard. "So
I'm pregnant. So Jason and I weren't all that careful all the time.
So what? What business is it of yours," she demanded.

"Ordinarily, none. But, Courtney, you and Jason didn't have to
be careful. Jason couldn't have children, could he?"

Without any warning her tumbler flew across the room and
smashed against the opposite wall, close to where Tommy Zito was
sitting. Both men were on their feet in a flash, Tommy's hair glistening with wine and shards of glass and Phillip moving toward
Courtney. But she was as quick as they were, bolting off the sofa to
the far end of the room where she spun round to confront them.
"You bastards! How *dare* you," she shrieked, "how dare you bring
your filth in here! How can you even suggest—I *loved* him! I
would've died for Jason . . . Just because you're too goddamn stupid to find his killer, you come here to persecute me! To make
something beautiful seem *dirty* . . . and you know nothing, nothing! This is his child and it's all I have left."

Courtney's fury ended in a flood of tears and Phillip, faced with
the genuineness of her distress, was again filled with doubt. College
was a long time ago, and people liked to tell stories about people,
especially about Saylin, even when he was still just Ainsly Drucker.
He cursed himself for not getting confirmation about Saylin's steril-

ity from another source and for placing himself in this untenable position. Attempting to make the best of a bad situation, he went over and laid a tentative hand on Courtney's quaking shoulder.

"I'm sorry, Courtney. I wasn't accusing you of anything. But I *have* to know the facts. I have to know if anyone had a reason for wanting Jason out of the way . . . if anyone was jealous of him because of you. You understand?"

Slowly she raised her tear-drenched face to his. The anger was gone now, but the bitterness remained. "Yes, I understand alright . . . better'n you do. You're lookin' for jealousy . . . and strychnine, right? Well, go take a look at your old pal, Andre. He had *both* in spades!"

It was his turn to freeze now. "What are you saying?"

She fretfully wiped a tear away with the sleeve of her kimono, leaving a trail of mascara beneath one eye. "I'm sayin', Mr. Gerrard, that you can buy *anything* down in Mexico. I'm sayin' that Andre has been known to like a little strych for his . . . 'bed games.' It's an Old World taste, you know. *And* I'm sayin'—and I was a fool not to mention it sooner—that the night Jason died, he and Andre had one hell of a row right before the guests arrived!" Upset but not blind, she caught the dubious looked which flickered across Phillip's face and read his thoughts. "Oh, I can just bet what you're thinkin'. Well, I'm *not* makin' it up. You go ask one of the hired help we had in that night, they'll tell you. Or Patsy can! She stopped by to lend me some glasses. Andre and Jason were in the study, but we could hear the ruckus clear in the kitchen."

"What were they fighting about?"

"I don't know . . . I told you we were in the kitchen! And I didn't have a chance to ask Jason later. I only caught Andre yelling somethin' about 'artistic integrity'—one of his pet subjects, so I didn't think much of it at the time."

"And what do you think of it now?"

She folded her arms and regarded the two men icily. "I don't think anything—nothin' at all. I just know someone killed my Jason . . . I leave it to you all to put two and two together."

CHAPTER XXI

"Where the *hell* have you been?!"

"Well, it's nice to see you, too, Ruth," Jocelyn panted, stumbling into the foyer of Merle Pelham's rambling old apartment on West End Avenue with a hastily gift-wrapped package under one arm. "Where are we stashing the loot?"

"On the coffee table in the living room. Do you realize it's past five-thirty?"

"Yes, I realize. I plan to make a novena. Just let me say 'hi' to Merle first." Jocelyn adroitly slipped past Ruth, catching the signs in her friend's implacable glare which stated clearly 'I'm not through with you yet!' and making her way toward the living room.

Merle, gargantuan with child and resplendent in a silver silk caftan, was gleefully presiding over a bar cart, mixing up a lethal looking batch of banana daiquiris. Seeming to derive a contact high just from handling the bottles, she waved expansively to Jocelyn. *"There* you are! We were afraid the white slavers got you. You look bushed. Here, have a belt." She extended a large, foamy glass. "Pick you right up. You'll need the lift. We're going to play Name the Babe later."

Jocelyn warily accepted the cocktail. She wasn't fond of sweet drinks and her parched throat wanted nothing but a nice cold beer. But the look of vicarious anticipation in Merle's face brooked no refusal. Taking a tentative sip and suppressing a grimace, she asked, "How do we play that? Draw up three columns for Him, Her or It?"

"Oh, nooo! Much easier," Merle said with a shake of her fuzzy, ash-blond locks, "It's a Him. Didn't Ruthie tell you? I had amniocentesis. Wanted to be on the safe side. It's a boy for sure. Now, all we have to do is come up with a name impressive enough to keep

Hervé from naming it after his grandfather. I'll be damned if any kid of mine's going through life called *Xavier!*"

"I'm with you all the way, Merle—even if it takes all night." And she meant it. Merle's husband, Hervé Ramos, was a brilliantly successful publicist from an old and moneyed Argentinian family. A man of great charm and easy urbanity, his taste in theatre and P.R. ran to the "now" and the "happening," but his taste in domestic matters was still firmly entrenched in the "then" and the "traditional." If she was going to have any say in the naming of their first child, Merle would need all the help she could get.

"Jocelyn O'Roarke. *Just* the woman I wanted to see!"

A bony hand reached out and spun her around by the elbow. She found herself face to angular face with Maxine Knox, whom she hadn't seen since the night of Saylin's ill-fated party. Jocelyn had always considered Maxine the inspiration for the old theatrical joke that went, "Why won't sharks eat agents? . . . Professional courtesy." Her appearance at such an intimate gathering was obviously a political move on Merle's part; Maxine handled some of Hervé's more celebrated clients.

Dragging her toward an overstuffed love seat, Maxine said, "This is such a relief. Ever since that awful, awful night, I've needed to *share* the experience with a fellow witness. You can't imagine how it's haunted me. Knowing how close you are to the whole thing, I'd really love to hear your thoughts on it."

"I'm sure you would. Will you settle for ten percent of my thoughts?" She didn't even bother to keep the asperity out of her tone, but Maxine, who had been snubbed by the best of them, was too avid to pay any notice.

"Now, don't be coy, Jocelyn. You're not talking to Earl Wilson, here. It's not for the record. I'm just very concerned . . . about people."

Jocelyn had a shrewd idea which "people" she meant. Courtney Mason had once been one of Maxine's clients. Unimpressed by Courtney's track record prior to her engagement to Saylin, Maxine had severed their professional connection. She was now obviously bent on lapping up spilled milk. Too tired to take the long way around Robin's red barn, Jocelyn said, "Don't worry, Maxine, I don't think Courtney's negotiating with anyone for the film rights to her story yet."

"Ouch. That's not fair, Josh." The muscles in Maxine's face twitched as much as two face jobs would let them. "This isn't business. I'm just afraid for Courtney."

"Well, don't be. Between the pharmacist and the liquor store, she's well protected. Besides, Patsy's looking after her."

"Oh, Patsy," Maxine said with a dismissive shrug of her lean shoulders. "Of course, Patsy'll *always* be there."

"Why 'of course'?"

"Don't tell me you don't *know*," the other woman asked smugly, "Why, Patsy brought Courtney to New York! Spotted her in a regional revival of *Tobacco Road* about ten years ago and convinced her to try the Big Apple. Courtney told me all about it. Said Patsy started out as a big-sister figure, then quickly became mother superior. I don't think Courtney was able to get out from under her thumb until she moved in with Jason."

Sensing that Maxine was baiting an elaborate hook for her, Jocelyn was nonetheless on the verge of biting when Ruth marched into the living room, wearing a frown and a chef's apron. "I need some help with the hors d'oeuvres, Josh!"

The request was too pointed to be ignored, and Jocelyn dutifully followed her friend into the kitchen. Ruth handed her a can of anchovies and pointed her toward the electric can opener before demanding, "What gives?"

"Maxine's last face-lift—within a year, if I'm any judge."

A celery stalk hit the wall inches above Jocelyn's head and bounced off onto the tile floor. She spun round to find Ruth brandishing a long rubber spatula with a threatening look in her eye. "I know you can't help being a wiseass, Josh—with you, it's an involuntary reflex. And I will admit that, since her last face job, Maxine *has* begun to resemble a promo for *The Mask of Fu Manchu*, but that is not the issue. The issue is, you've gone very cloak-and-dagger on me today and I can't *stand* it! For cripes' sake, what's going on?!"

Appalled by her own lack of sensitivity, Jocelyn bent down to retrieve the celery stalk. Ruth was not, by nature, a flinger of food. Quite the contrary, and she would be driven to such an act only by another's extreme obtuseness. Their friendship was founded on a mutual obsession which they referred to as "the need to know." Apologetically, Jocelyn asked, "Where do you want me to start?"

"With 'the man and the book' story. *What* man and *what* book?"

As succinctly as possible, Jocelyn began describing her interview with Franklin Allen while Ruth calmed herself down by whipping up a tray of deviled eggs. The calm was short lived. With each sentence Ruth's normally sleepy eyes grew as large and round as the hard-boiled eggs she was arranging on a silver platter.

"Holy moly! You really *said* that?! Gave him that whole campaign for ousting Irene," Ruth squeaked, trying to keep her shock from ebbing into the next room, "and he bought it? What balls. You know, Josh, underhanded and diabolical as it was, it's still the best sales pitch you've ever done for yourself."

"Sad but true," she said with a wince. "Unfortunately, it takes a major felony to get me motivated."

"Anyway, how did you get from that to asking Franklin to lend you Andre's book?"

"Well, I . . . uh . . . didn't, really," Jocelyn said, making herself very busy with the can of anchovies. "Franklin had to get back to rehearsal so I sort of . . . took it."

"You *stole* his book," Ruth gasped.

"No! I *borrowed* it . . . without telling him."

"Why?"

"I needed to check something. Here—look at this." Jocelyn dove into her bag and pulled out Allen's copy of *Lost Ladies.* She opened it to the page with the bracketed paragraph and scribbled notation. Ruth scanned the page, absentmindedly sprinkling paprika over the eggs, and then looked up. "I don't get it. What's the big deal about an ex-movie queen named Fenton?"

"Who knows? I'm still not sure. But look at what's written in the margin!"

"I'm looking, I'm just not understanding," Ruth whispered plaintively, staring as hard as she could at "Ck. vs. S. rev. for 'F. Flowers', '79" and waiting for enlightenment.

"Come on, Ruthie! It's not so tough. Check against S. rev.—my guess is that means 'Saylin's review.'"

"You sure?" Ruth, ever the doubting Thomas, asked.

"I am now. I spent hours in the Fifth Avenue library after I left the Above Boards today. After much moaning and gnashing of teeth, I tracked down a review that Jason wrote for *Metropolitan Magazine* in March of seventy-nine for an ill-fated show called *Faded Flowers*, starring, among others . . . Gladys Fenton!"

"Whew! What did it say?"

"I'm not sure."

"What the—? After going to all that trouble?!"

"Look, after going to all that trouble, it was nearly four-thirty and the Xerox machine was broken! I had to dredge up the remnants of my high-school shorthand course and copy the review into my notebook. Then I dashed home to change, wrap my gift . . . and check my messages. But that's another ugly story. I haven't really had a chance to go over the review yet!"

Empathizing with her friend's frustration, Ruth shook her head and murmured, "That's a bitch," just as the kitchen door swung open and Maxine Knox poked her head in, trilling, "Girls, it's gift time!"

CHAPTER XXII

One of Tommy Zito's biggest assets was knowing when to keep his mouth shut. Ever since Gerrard walked out of Courtney Mason's apartment building looking more incensed than Ricardo Montalban in *The Wrath of Khan*, Tommy hadn't said a word. He'd barely had time to shut the squad car door before Phillip tore away from the curb and flipped on the siren, something he rarely did. After that, conversation had been out of the question.

It wasn't until they were halfway across Central Park that Zito, miming a migraine, persuaded Gerrard to shut off the siren and state their destination.

"So, we're going to see Guérisseur, huh? I kinda figured that," Tommy said, warming up to the topic he'd wanted to broach for the last twenty minutes. "Hey, Phil, what Mason said about strychnine—is that for real?"

Still caught up in a private bout of self-recrimination, Gerrard snapped, "Is *what* for real? You'll have to be more specific, since I'm not a goddamn mind reader!"

"Oh, not the stuff about him picking it up while they were in Mexico. She was pretty steamed up and probably talkin' through her hat. I mean, what she said about him using it as a aphro——, whad ya call it . . . using it to get a rise in the rack, you know."

"Having never tried it, I wouldn't know," Phillip said with a grim smile. "Look, I told you about that textbook case I read where the kid's mother used it as an aphrodisiac, but it didn't include her testament to strych as a turn-on. All this stuff you hear about different sexual enhancers, most scientists say it's just guff, but that doesn't mean that people don't still try them."

"Do you think Guérisseur's one of those people?"

Releasing a deep sigh, he shook his head and said, "To tell you the truth, I really don't know." It was bearing down on him with great force exactly how much he *didn't* know about Andre. In college he had known him as a man with a subtle and brilliant mind and an amorphous ego. But even then, in the first throes of his own libidinous urgings, he had given very little thought to Andre as a male animal with his own drives and passions trapped within a stunted body. Because he had always regarded Andre as a supremely civilized man, it pained him acutely to realize that, during the course of this investigation, he had fallen prey to the very same personal biases for which he had so righteously castigated Jocelyn.

Parking in front of a fire hydrant, another uncharacteristic move, he marched into the lobby of Andre's building with Zito following on his heels. Standing by a small mahogany desk in the foyer was a Hispanic doorman, wearing a braided uniform and peaked cap with the assurance of a successful junta general.

"Where you going, please," he asked with a toothsome smile.

"Up to Penthouse B, to see Mr. Guérisseur."

With a stately nod, he picked up the intercom phone and buzzed the penthouse. After buzzing a second and third time, he replaced the receiver with great aplomb and announced, "Too bad. He's no home. You wanna leave a message?"

Tommy Zito's second biggest asset was his ability to read things turned upside down and backward. Glancing at the book on the doorman's desk, he observed, "He was home an hour ago. You let somebody up then. I can't make out the name but it says 'Penthouse B' . . . Has he gone out since then?"

To add weight to Tommy's question, Phillip flipped out his badge and watched the general retreat. "Ah, no—I don't see him leave. Maybe he asleep," he asked hopefully.

"Then, maybe we'll wake him," Gerrard said, moving toward the elevators, picking up a whiff of marijuana emanating from the doorman on the way. "Who did you let up earlier?"

Obviously a victim of too many *Kojack* reruns, the uniformed man's eyes widened as he stammered, "I no—just some lady. Big woman in sunglasses."

"Did you see her leave?"

"No, no, I was havin' a . . . cigarette outside. I dinna see nothin'."

Following Phillip into the elevator, Zito looked over his shoulder and grunted, "Smoke got in your eyes?"

The elevator ascended to the top floor without a halt, which was a blessing as far as Gerrard was concerned. At some point, down in the lobby, his nose had started twitching with a vengeance. It suddenly became very urgent to him to get inside that apartment and get to Andre.

Like a bad dream come true, Phillip's repeated ringing of the doorbell brought no response from within. Starting to pound on the door with one hand, certain that he heard some kind of commotion inside, he grabbed Tommy's arm with the other and gave him a light shove in the direction of the still-open elevator.

"Get back downstairs and dig up a key to this door. I don't care what you have to do to get it! I'm going up to the roof and see if there's a way in from there. Hurry!"

The two men split off in opposite directions, Phillip heading for the fire exit. Without looking back, Zito shouted, "Phil—be careful! That terrace is all *glass.*"

"Not for long, it isn't," Gerrard muttered to himself, charging up a flight of cement stairs. "The nose *knows.*"

CHAPTER XXIII

"Ooh, Josh. I just *love* this mobile," Merle enthused, lifting it out of the tissue paper and tossing the box on a small mountain of refuse by her chair. "It's the height of infant chic. Where did you find it?"

"Actually, I commissioned Louise Nevelson to do it. She's branching out to crib sculpture these days," Jocelyn said amiably. Despite her itching desire to get back to Andre's book and the transcription of Saylin's review, she couldn't help but be touched by her friend's boundless delight, which had only grown with the unveiling of each new gift. Jocelyn's was the last in a long line. Remembering her sister's first pregnancy, she realized that Merle's high spirits were probably an outlet for the prenatal willies, but that was only to be expected. Laying the mobile gently aside, Merle clapped her hands and chimed, "Okay, everybody, now it's time to Name the Babe! Could somebody go into the bedroom and get my *Dictionary of Names?* The little sadist kicks like hell every time I stand up."

She didn't have to ask twice. Jocelyn was on her feet and halfway down the hall before anyone else could volunteer, glad for the excuse to get out of the room for a few minutes. A half hour of listening to maternity stories and endless theories about child rearing had set her teeth on edge. Having been an aunt since the age of eleven, she knew quite a bit about the practical realities of raising children, enough to know that it was a wonderful and rewarding experience . . . for some people. For herself, she was perfectly content to play the Auntie Mame role for life. It was a firm conviction that she seldom voiced, having learned that it only brought pitying glances and inane speculations about "maternal displacement" from most people.

Like an unnecessary office memo, the first thing she spotted walking into Merle and Hervé's snug and sybaritic bedroom was a copy of *People* magazine on the nightstand, which was opened to a story about Jason's mysterious demise. The article featured a photo of Saylin and Courtney attending the Tony awards with the predictable caption, "In happier days." Something in the picture caught Jocelyn's eye, something familiar, and she leaned over to examine it more closely. It wasn't just the faces; Courtney looked uncommonly relaxed and happy and Saylin typically smug and effete with an overcoat thrown, à la Gordon Craig, over the shoulders of his tuxedo. It was something else. "Oh, of course, that's it," she said aloud to no one, "it's the *cane!*"

Tipped jauntily over Jason's left shoulder was an antique cane, the twin of which she'd seen the night she visited Andre. Unconsciously her hand delved into her shoulder bag and extracted *Lost Ladies* with a will of its own. Seeing the cane had triggered off something in the far recesses of her brain, and she felt compelled to examine the book again. The bubbling flow of conversation from the next room assured her that she wouldn't be missed for a few minutes, and she quickly flipped to the page with the bracketed paragraph, which read:

> Like many of her celluloid compatriots, Gladys Fenton was unable to make the transition from nubile ingenue to femme fatale or even character actress, lacking the incessant electricity of a Bette Davis or the mature assurance of a Mary Astor. The poor box office response to her "breakthrough" film, *Lady of the Evening*, made it portentiously plain that her public only wanted to see her as the girl next door, not as the girl upstairs. Overtaken by the ineluctably inevitable, Miss Fenton followed in the footsteps of fellow failures and wisely opted for a successful abdication (via marriage to a Dow Jones doyen). Serenely sebaceous, the former "Glad Girl" now lives in Connecticut, where she has replaced her fervent fans with a coterie of canines—prizewinning Shih Tzus, to be exact. Showing greater adaptability in her life than in her art, Gladys, the consummate show girl, has tidily taken off the tinsel by putting on the dog.

With a vague sense of déjà vu, she was about to reread the passage when Maxine Knox bellowed from the living room, "Jocelyn, where's the damn dictionary?"

Making a quick detour through the kitchen, she rejoined the gathering with a cold Molson in one hand and the dictionary in the other, which she assiduously kept charge of for the sake of camouflage. The setup was far from ideal, but, with the oversized paperback in her lap and her open notebook inside it, she could read out the meaning of names while trying to decipher her transcription of Jason's review at the same time. It was a long time since high-school theology class, when she'd kept a copy of *Splendour in the Grass* inside her New Testament, and she was a little rusty at it. But no one seemed to notice—except Ruth, of course, who was sitting on an ancient ottoman, aglow with inquisitiveness.

"How about Fabian," someone ventured. "Fabian Ramos has a nice, sexy ring to it."

"Uh . . . Fabian," Jocelyn repeated, flipping to the *f*'s, "from the Latin . . . 'bean grower.'"

A chorus of moans and boos went around the room as Jocelyn made out the headline on the review—*"Faded Flowers* Drops Its Petals"—a typical Saylin sally, indicative of worse things to come. The first paragraph referred to "an expiring new playwright" and a director "too inept to direct traffic at a school crosswalk" but made no mention of Gladys Fenton.

"I like Gordon," a svelte young dancer, sitting in a lotus position on the rug, cooed. "Dated a guy with that name in college. He had the most *amazing*—"

"Gordon, huh," Jocelyn cut in, "Okay . . . let's see—'name of a famous Scottish clan, the Gay Gordons—meaning uncertain.'"

"Not to Hervé, I'm afraid," Merle said with a dismissive shrug. "He's from the 'as the twig is bent so grows the tree' school of thinking."

A third pitcher of daiquiris was making the rounds and names started flying fast and furiously, followed just as quickly by Merle's various objections. In between, Jocelyn had scant time for perusal.

"What about Jared?"

"From the Hebrew . . . 'descent.'"

"Meaning 'it's just downhill from here, kid'? Nope."

"Well, Merle, you're part Irish. How about Moran? What does that mean, Josh?"

"Uh . . . 'hairy.' "

"That's gross."

"Preston sounds classy."

"Teutonic . . . means 'priest's dwelling.' "

"I *don't* think so."

During a lively debate over Barry, "straight shooter," versus Luke, "light," Jocelyn hastened back to her notes and, much to her surprise, spotted a familiar name. In her agitation to get the whole thing copied down at the library, she'd put her mind on hold and wrote like an automaton. But there on the page in front of her, in her own concise script, was Patsy Snell's name, listed as lighting designer on *Faded Flowers* and faring no better with Saylin than had her cohorts. "Ms. Snell comes to Broadway via the world of grand opera, and it shows. She has chosen to light a realistic, do-mestic drama as if it were the last act of *La Bohème.* One also wonders if she ordered all her gels direct from the island of Lesbos, as she has contrived to make all the women look like amber angels, which wouldn't be so bad if all the men didn't resemble cigar-store redskins."

She was just coming to the section on Gladys Fenton when Merle asked, "What about Richard, Josh? Richard Ramos has a nice, strong sound to it."

Before she could turn to the *r*'s, Ruth said. "Wait a second. There's already a Richard Ramos in Actors Equity. If the kid grows up to be an actor—a grim thought, but all too likely—he'll have to change his name."

"Oh, my gosh, I hadn't thought of that," Merle said, cradling her extended belly. "What if he wants to be an *actor?!*"

This lead to a flurry of opinions on the best way to raise a child in a show-biz family, an age-old topic among theatre women, but Jocelyn wasn't listening. With the pressure of time her writing had become increasingly scrawled, but certain phrases floated up from the page and echoed disturbingly in her mind—"Sadly, the Glad Girl's comeback is a comedown . . . Fenton, never successful in character parts, has become a caricature actress . . . Her Rose is more like a porcine peony going to seed before our very eyes." It was Saylin's usual brand of vintage venom, but with a difference; at least it seemed that way to Jocelyn. She felt as if she had been staring for a very long time at a painting held upside down and someone was just beginning to right the canvas, but before the picture could come into focus Maxine's gravelly voice rose above the others. "Well, Merle, if you don't want the kid to become an actor, why not name him after a critic. Call him Jason."

All conversation came to an abrupt halt, save for a few gasps and a stifled giggle or two. If Maxine had intended to be witty, her plan had severely backfired, or maybe it was just the effects of her fourth daiquiri, or maybe mere spite. In any case Merle gave her a look worthy of Queen Victoria and said, "I never cared for that name." Her subtext clearly read, "And we are *not* amused." From where she sat, Jocelyn distinctly heard Ruth mutter, "I never cared for that dame." On her best days Ruth considered agents a necessary evil. On other days, they were just plain evil.

To ease the tension in the room Jocelyn said, "Hell, if you were going to saddle an innocent child with a critic's name, better to call him Brooks."

"Right—or Walter," Ruth chimed in.

Someone else said, "Or even—yech—Clive."

"Or Frank or Harold," was another choice.

"Or Marilyn," Merle said in a perfect deadpan voice, ending the round and convulsing the group with laughter. With the party on the upswing again, Jocelyn covertly flipped through the dictionary until she came to the *j*'s. Tasteless as Maxine's suggestion was, it had kindled an obscure curiosity within her. After all, Jason wasn't his real name; he must have had some reason for choosing it, she thought. The entry read, "Jason (Greek)—'healer.'"

"Holy Christ! 'Healer'—it means 'healer,'" she shouted. Twelve pairs of questioning eyes flew in her direction, but Jocelyn was totally oblivious as she yanked Andre's book from her bag to examine the flyleaf inscription once again. "To Ainsly—and a new beginning, From Andre." She leapt up from her seat, letting the dictionary fall to the floor with a heavy thud.

"Merle, I need a dictionary."

"There's one at your feet," Maxine observed sourly.

Jocelyn didn't even hear her. "You took that Berlitz course before you and Hervé went to Cannes last year, right?"

"Sure, for all the good it did me," Merle said. "But why—"

"Do you have a French-English dictionary?"

Something in Jocelyn's face made Merle omit the next why.

"Uh-huh, it's in the bedroom, on the top shelf of the bookcase."

Five minutes later, Jocelyn had found the dictionary and what she wanted from it. A staggering premise was forming in her mind and with it a myriad of ramifications. The canvas had righted itself and assumed its true perspective, but it was all unsubstantiated. She needed something concrete, she needed . . . Phillip.

Reaching for the bedside phone, she stabbed the buttons with ferocious urgency and cursed under her breath while the number rang.

"Lieutenant Gerrard's office. Detective Fallon speaking."

"Fallon? Oh, yes, Jerry," she said, momentarily disconcerted. "Is the lieutenant in? This is Jocelyn O'Roarke."

"No. I'm afraid he's not," Fallon replied in his most officious manner. "Can I take a message?"

"No, no . . . Is Sergeant Zito there, then?"

"Zito's with the lieutenant, Miss O'Roarke," he answered silkily. "Can I be of any help?"

"Well, can you tell me where they are? Where I can reach him?" she asked, trying to keep the desperation out of her voice.

"Uh . . . I don't think"—Fallon hesitated—"He can't be reached. It wouldn't be advisable."

"*Bugger* what's advisable! Listen, Fallon, this isn't a goddamn social call. It's about the Saylin case and I have to talk to Phillip right away! It's *important,* you little twer——" She bit off the last words but succeeded in making her point.

"Okay, okay, calm down," he said, sounding more agitated every second. "I just didn't want to upset you, Miss O'Roarke."

"You've already blown that. Where *is* he?"

"Zito phoned in a minute ago. The lieutenant's at the Lenox Hill Hospital with Andre Guérisseur . . . They've both just been admitted to the emergency room."

CHAPTER XXIV

"Two inches higher and a little deeper in and he would've been in big trouble," the young, lanky intern said, squinting with fatigue down at Tommy Zito. "All in all, he was pretty damn lucky. Now, the other guy . . . well, it's too soon to tell. Could go either way."

"Sure, sure, but when will you know?"

Before the intern could answer, the door of the waiting room flew open. Looking both disheveled and incongruously elegant in a mauve velour dress and high heels, Jocelyn spotted Zito and made a beeline for him. In one hand, Tommy noticed, she carried a paperback dictionary; the other she laid on his arm while gazing at his face with wide, beseeching eyes. It took her a moment to speak, and Tommy realized that she was struggling to get hold of herself. He'd seen the look before on the faces of hundreds of terrified policemen's wives, but to see it on Jocelyn's face was, somehow, even more unbearable. It held all the helpless fear that he'd been repressing for the last two hours.

When she finally spoke, it was only two hushed words. "How bad?"

Without thinking, he put his arm around her shoulders in a tight grip and said, "It's alright, Josh, really . . . We had to break into Andre's place. Phil got cut on some glass but he's gonna be fine, swear to God! Just fine."

She looked up at the suddenly alert intern, who nodded his confirmation. She then pressed both her palms over her eyes and shook silently for a moment. Both men watched warily as she brought her hands away from her face, bracing themselves for a flood of hysterics, but all she said was, "How soon can I see him?"

Shocked out of his bedside manner, the doctor said, "Oh . . . um . . . in about five minutes, I guess. He's been stitched up and given a transfusion. They should be taking him up to his room about now. You can go up with the sergeant, but you'll have to keep it short. The painkillers are going to hit him in about twenty minutes and he'll need to rest."

On the way up to the fifth floor Tommy filled her in on the scene that had taken place at the penthouse. "When Andre didn't answer the door, Phil was sure something was wrong. He sent me down to get a master key and went up to the roof. There was a cinder block up there that he dropped through the glass roof of the terrace. Then he tied his coat to a rail on the wall and dropped over the ledge. His aim was pretty good, but it's about fifteen feet from the roof to the terrace. A piece of glass caught him in the chest on the way down . . . but he made it."

Appalled by the matter-of-factness of Zito's tone, she forced her mind to focus on specifics and kept her voice in a normal register. "Swell. Then what happened?"

"By the time I got back up there, Phil had the door open and was in the bathroom with Andre . . . trying to get him to vomit. Geez, that was awful. Phil was bleeding like a stuck pig and we weren't sure *what* Guérisseur had taken, but it was a clear suicide attempt. He was twitching like a dyin' cockroach. Phil wouldn't even wait for an ambulance. We got in the squad car and radioed ahead to the hospital. I didn't know if we were gonna make it in time. Hell, I still don't know if we did!"

"Andre's that bad?"

"Looks that way. They're still pumping him out."

They came off the elevator and turned down a long corridor. Approaching the room, Jocelyn felt a tight knot forming in the pit of her stomach. She had barely recovered from the dozen nightmare visions which had tormented her on the way to the hospital, the product of a remorseful and overactive imagination. Her prime fear now laid to rest, her mind was free to fret over a host of other worries, not the least of which was whether Phillip would be glad to see her and willing to listen to what she had to say. Sensing her hesitation, Zito preceded her into the room, only to be greeted by Gerrard's irate bark. "Where the hell have you been? Goddamn hospitals. I *told* them I wanted to see you right away. Have they found anything yet?"

"I think so. Martinez is on his way down here. Now, just relax, Phil . . . Josh is here."

She crept around Tommy and approached the bed with a shy smile. "Hi, sailor. Come here often?"

Propped up in bed, with his chest swaddled in gauze and his face looking like someone had played tic-tac-toe on it with a rusty nail, Phillip gave the remarkable impression of a man feeling absolutely no pain. His hand reached out for hers. "Sure t'ing, sister. Youse meet all the best people dat way."

From the far corner of the room Zito watched as Jocelyn eased herself onto the edge of the bed and brushed a fallen lock of hair from Phillip's forehead. Nothing more was said, but as they sat there, gazing at each other, Tommy had the definite feeling that a very long conversation was taking place nonetheless.

Finally, Phillip asked, "Did Tommy tell you about Andre?" Jocelyn nodded. "He said he tried to kill himself but he didn't say how."

Gerrard leaned back to stare glumly up at the ceiling and sighed, "Strychnine. He swallowed strychnine. The doctors just confirmed it. But we still don't know *why*. I've got a team of men going over the whole penthouse right now, looking for—"

There was a sharp rap on the door, and a young rookie cop with a solemn face and intelligent brown eyes came in holding a manila envelope. "Martinez. What've you got?" Gerrard asked, trying to raise himself up in bed, then thinking better of it.

"Just what you told us to look for, lieutenant," Martinez said, handing the envelope over. "It was on the desk in the study—short but sweet."

Jocelyn watched as Phillip drew out a sheet of cream-colored vellum stationery, encased in plastic. He studied it for a long moment, his eyes narrowed to slits and a stormy look clouding his countenance.

"Checked this for prints?"

"Yes, sir. It only shows Guérisseur's, no one else's."

"Handwriting?"

"Can't be certain yet. But we matched it with some other samples in the apartment. Either it's his or a really brilliant forgery."

"Alright, how about that visitor Andre had this afternoon. Any leads on who the woman might be?"

"No, sir, not yet," Martinez answered, wiping a thin film of perspiration from his upper lip. "We're still working on it."

"Work harder," Gerrard shot back. "I want *all* the facts before we move on this. Tommy, get down to the lab and get the analysis on the kind of strych Andre took. Beat it out of them if you have to and no screwups this time! I want to hear from both of you within the hour."

"But, Phil," Tommy protested, "the doctors said—"

"The doctors can go stuff themselves," Phillip exploded. "I want some action on this—*now!*"

Both men bolted out of the room, leaving Jocelyn to restrain their superior officer. Phillip fell back on the pillows, breathing heavily, a cold sweat breaking out on his forehead. He looked far worse than he had fifteen minutes ago, and she guessed that his pain was more than purely physical. She held her peace and waited until he listlessly handed her the note. It was addressed to Phillip with that day's date at the top and below, in elegantly flowing script, was one simple line—"I killed Jason Saylin." It was signed, "Andre Guérisseur."

Sadly, Jocelyn looked down at Merle's French dictionary, which she still held in her left hand. Instead of shocking her, Andre's note only confirmed what she had already discovered within its dog-eared pages. Glancing up, she saw the silent denial in Phillip's eyes and gently leaned forward to stroke his cheek, saying, "This is no forgery, love. Andre wrote it . . . and it's the truth."

CHAPTER XXV

There was a policeman standing guard outside Andre Guérisseur's hospital room by the time Jocelyn wheeled Gerrard out of the elevator onto the ninth floor. After waging a battle royal with the truculent head nurse, who was determined to keep him in bed, he had finally gained his freedom when an abnormally demure Jocelyn had promised to keep him off his feet and in the wheelchair. Once they were out of hearing range she stilled his grumblings by explaining, "Some nurses are like nuns—firmly convinced that they're on a mission from God. They're like human altars and you can't get around 'em without making a pro forma genuflection to their 'divine reason.' Of this, I am sure, believe me."

"I believe you," he said grudgingly. "Now, how sure are you of your theory about Andre?"

"Ninety-five percent," she answered unhesitatingly. "I'll know for certain when I see Franklin."

Drawing abreast of the beefy middle-aged cop, Phillip asked, "How's it going, Garvas. Any news?"

"Nope. No change so far. The doc's in there now. How're you doing, lieutenant? Hear you had a rough day."

"Yeah—ruined my best jacket," Gerrard grunted, pushing open the door.

Just inside the door, the young intern Jocelyn had met earlier with Zito was examining a bed chart while he absentmindedly tied a knot in his stethoscope. A few feet away, a gray-haired nurse with thick ankles stood adjusting the I.V. which dripped into the patient's limp arm.

Jocelyn looked at the man lying in the bed, then quickly looked away. She had seen illness before and even death, but never this— the aftermath of self-inflicted violence. Unconscious and laboring for breath, with a thin trail of spittle coming out the side of his mouth, Andre looked pathetically like a clubbed seal adrift on a snowy linen ice floe. It was heartrending to think that he had brought himself to this sorry and demeaned state.

Catching sight of Phillip, the lanky medic—whose name tag read: "B. Hadley"—opened his mouth, ready to take up scolding where the head nurse had left off. He was nipped in the bud by Gerrard's upraised hand and brusque inquiry. "Is he going to make it?"

Taken aback, he sputtered, "I . . . um . . . we don't know yet. He's been pumped clean and the sedatives have taken effect. The convulsions have stopped, for the time being, anyway. But there are still a lot of variables involved."

"I don't want variables. I want the odds. What are his chances?"

From firsthand experience Jocelyn knew that Phillip's rapid-fire tactics usually got results. But Hadley, who looked exhausted and harried past endurance, wasn't having any. He shot a concerned glance toward his patient. Then, in a swift and unexpected movement, he grabbed the handles of the wheelchair and pushed Gerrard back out into the hallway, with Jocelyn following close behind. Once outside, Hadley rubbed at his five-o'clock shadow and addressed the detective in a hoarse whisper. "Look, mister, I don't know who the hell you think you're dealing with, but let me enlighten you—I'm *not* young Dr. Kildare! I have no pat answers for you. For Pete's sake, we don't even see that many strychnine cases in the course of a year, and they're certainly nothing like this! That guy had nearly a gram of the stuff in him. By rights, he should be as dead as a doornail already. If you hadn't gotten him in here so fast, he definitely would be. Frankly, I'm flabbergasted by his resistance. He seems to have some kind of built-in immunity to the poison!"

"He *does?*" Despite her firm resolve to keep mum, Jocelyn gasped with amazement.

"Yeah . . . I expected that," Phillip muttered.

"You *did?* But why—" He cut short her question with a wave of the hand and turned back to the towheaded intern, who seemed nearly as dumbfounded by his remark as Jocelyn. In a far more amenable tone, he said, "Listen, Hadley, I'm sorry I came on like Bulldog Drummond just now. I realize that you've been working like a son of a bitch to save him. You must be beat. I don't blame you for rolling my keester out of there."

"Oh, heck, I didn't mind . . . I mean, that's not why I did it," Hadley said with an amiable grin. "I was concerned for Mr. Guérisseur. You see, in his condition any stimulus—a loud noise or a touch, even—can set off another convulsion. That's why the room has to be kept dark and quiet. Death generally occurs during a seizure. The patient suffocates."

Jocelyn didn't think it was possible, but Phillip actually turned a shade whiter upon hearing this. "Jesus—I'm a jackass! I could've—"

As a diversionary tactic and to satisfy her own growing curiosity, she butted in a second time. "What I don't understand is why Saylin died so quickly. He couldn't have taken in nearly as much as Andre and he was dead within an hour!"

"Oh, the Saylin case! I read about it," Hadley said, brightening. "But that was different, Miss . . . um?"

"O'Roarke. Call me Jocelyn. Nice to meet you, doctor."

"Same here . . . and it's Ben." He extended a long arm to shake her hand and she was ineffably charmed to see him blush. "See, from what I gather, Saylin was an epileptic. That would make him more susceptible. Secondly, he inhaled the stuff. Strychnine is absorbed through the mucous membranes, you understand. By snorting it, he got maximum impact in minimal time. It's no wonder he went so fast."

"Geez, Phil, you shouldn't be outa bed. What d'ya think you're doing?" Tommy Zito asked trundling down the hall with an anxious frown on his face. He stuffed the remains of a spinach and cheese calzone, his preferred mobile meal, into a paper sack. "Josh, why'd you let him—"

"Nothin' she could do about it, Thomas. The principal gave me a hall pass. You get the lab results?"

"Sorta'. You know Strohmier. He's a real stickler. Wants everything double-checked before he'll announce his findings. But I got him to 'commit to an opinion'—that's what he calls it, anyway."

"And what does the Great Von Stroh opine?"

"Weirdest thing, Phil," Tommy said scratching the back of his neck, "but he says it looks like the stuff that Guérisseur took *did* come from the bag of Mouse Maze out on the terrace. It's not the pure strych that Saylin got."

"Well, I'll be damned. Now, that's *very* interesting. Wouldn't you say so?" Phillip asked Jocelyn with a meaningful glance. She gave him an affirmative nod. Hadley looked on with unabashed schoolboy fascination as Zito rattled off the rest of his news.

"Another thing. I got ahold of one of the guys from Lend-A-Hand who worked at Saylin's party that night. Seems they use a lot of out-of-work actors, so you can bet this kid was paying attention to everything that went down. And Courtney Mason wasn't lyin'. Saylin and Andre did have a big blowup before the party started. This fella caught an earful while he was putting ashtrays around the living room. They were arguing about the review for *Hedda Gabler.* Andre said the show was a"—he paused to consult a pocket notebook—" 'A total travesty' and oughta' be panned, but Saylin was against it. What I can't figure is—"

Intuiting the rest of his question, Phillip cut him off by asking, "Did you reach Franklin Allen?"

Zito slapped his forehead with the palm of his hand. "Shit. I forgot. I mean, I called him. I just forgot to tell you that he's here. I met him on my way in. He's waiting down on the fifth floor in your room. And he's pretty upset. Wanted to come up here to see Guérisseur but I told him no dice. You want me to take you down there?"

"Nope. I can manage, thanks. You stay here for a bit and fill Jocelyn and the doc—Ben, I mean—in on what Courtney told us this afternoon," Phillip said, wheeling the chair in the direction of the elevator. "I want a few minutes alone with him. Then you can bring Josh down . . . Got it?"

Tommy wasn't at all sure that he did, but Gerrard wasn't waiting for an answer. He was already halfway down the corridor, wheeling himself at a steady clip. But the expression on Jocelyn's face, an amalgam of concern and determination, told him that she, at least, was cognizant of the game plan. It was obvious to Zito that she and Phillip had something up their collective sleeve, and it surprised him faintly to realize that he didn't resent this. On the contrary, he felt suddenly calm and reassured.

"Tommy, what Courtney said today—does it have any bearing

on Andre's tolerance for strychnine?" Jocelyn prodded as a new train of thought began racing through her mind.

"Oh, yeah, yeah, let me tell ya—" He stopped in mid sentence when he noticed Hadley rubbing the back of his neck. "What's the matter, doc? Got a crink?"

"You bet," Ben groaned. "Happens every time I work a double shift. The ol' neck stiffens up."

"Well, just take it easy and pull up a chair," Tommy said, flexing his fingers with professional pride. "Relief is on the way."

CHAPTER XXVI

"I just can't *understand* it! A suicide attempt—swallowing poison, no less. It's so dramatic, borders on the Elizabethan, really, which would make sense if it were someone like, oh, say, Courtney or Irene, God, yes, definitely Irene! I can just see her trying to commission Marsha Norman to write the farewell note. But *Andre?!* Well, I mean, it's so totally . . . out of character, don't you think?"

Franklin Allen ended his babbling on a feeble note and resumed gnawing on a thumbnail, leaving Phillip an opening into what had thus far been a one-sided conversation.

"I'm afraid I've seen too many suicides to have any fixed notions on who is or isn't the type. But as far as cases like this go—failed suicides, I mean—they generally fall into one of two categories: someone who genuinely miscalculated, or someone using desperate means to gain attention."

"Oh, well, I'd certainly put Andre in the former group, no question. He's designed his whole life so as to attract as little attention as possible. Being with Jason made it that much easier. No, if he set out to kill himself, you can believe he was—excuse the expression—dead serious."

"I think you're right, Franklin," Gerrard said easily, wheeling his chair a little closer to the end of the hospital bed where Allen was perched. "I was hoping you might have some idea why."

Startled, he sprung like a tightly wound jack-in-the-box off the bed and moved around the wheelchair, heading toward the window. "Why, what . . . what're you asking me?"

"The obvious—why would Andre try to take his own life?"

"But I just *told* you, I have *no* idea," he insisted in tones both plaintive and apprehensive. "I find the whole situation completely incomprehensible!"

"Now, come on, Franklin, you can do better than that," Phillip chided amiably. "You're a brilliant director. Just stop thinking in terms of 'character' and start thinking about 'motives' . . . like fear, desperation . . . blackmail."

Whirling away from the window, Allen found himself hedged into the far corner of the room by Phillip and his wheelchair. "Blackmail?! Who said anything about blackmail? Did Andre leave some kind of note, is that it?"

"As a matter of fact, he did. Care to make any guesses about its contents?"

For a good ten seconds the wiry little man held himself in tensile stillness, his eyes boring into Gerrard's while his mind seemed to wrestle with some secret chess game. Eventually he made his move and snapped back into kinetic overdrive. "No, I don't think I do, thank you. Whatever Andre's note said, I doubt seriously that it had anything to do with me. However, I applaud your virtuosity. You're doing *Ironsides* this time, right? Very effective, props and all. Too bad you're wheeling up the wrong ramp."

"Maybe it would help if I greased the wheels," Jocelyn asked cheerfully, standing in the doorway with her arms folded across her chest and Andre's book prominently displayed in the crook of her elbow. "Hi ya, Franklin. Read any good books lately?"

Strolling into the room in front of Tommy Zito, she kept her eyes glued on Allen's face, not wanting to miss even the briefest change of expression. He didn't give away much, but it was enough to make her sure of her bearings despite the studied nonchalance of his voice. "Well, well, if it isn't Jessica Tandy come to visit her wounded Hume Cronyn. While I'm handing out plaudits, I really must compliment you, Josh, on your stellar performance this morning. And all just to—and I use the term loosely—'borrow' a book."

"Oh, I know I probably could've gotten it from the library," she said with mock contriteness, hopping onto the now rumpled bed. "But then I would've missed out on your tremendously insightful notes. You know, about Gladys Fenton and Jason's review of *Faded Flowers.*"

"I don't see what's so insightful about that. I happen to be a fan of the Glad Girl from way back. I've always followed her career."

"And a good thing you did, eh? How else would you've tumbled to it?"

"I'm no acrobat and I haven't the faintest idea what you're talking about," he maintained with some asperity.

"Is that a fact," Jocelyn asked obliquely. "But you *did* read *Lost Ladies*. You must have some opinion about it?"

Acutely aware that all eyes were on him, Allen shrugged with irritation and adopted the air of a bored pedant. "*Lost Ladies* is little more than a hardbound fan magazine for confirmed film buffs. An affectionate, sometimes star-struck treatise, written by a bright but callow college boy."

"I couldn't agree with you more," she nodded emphatically. "But that's what's so interesting . . . about the Gladys Fenton section, I mean. After all that adoration, he gets a little rough with Ol' Gladys—and you have to wonder why, don't you? There's that undercurrent of snideness and all poor Gladys did was go back East and get *fat*."

"Well, writers, just like actors, have their own little idiosyncrasies."

"Exactly!" Jocelyn said, bent on agreeing Allen into a corner, "and their idiosyncrasies become part of their style, right? Remember that interview you did with *The Village Voice* where you said, 'Style is more than form, it's the psyche's signature'?"

"Vaguely," Allen muttered, "but I don't see the significance—"

"Like fun, you don't! It's one of your pet theories and it's why you bracketed that passage in Andre's book," she growled, yanking her notebook out of her purse and placing it alongside the book. "You saw a young writer with an antipathy for fleshy females, an inordinate fondness for alliterations—I mean, 'the ineluctably inevitable'? Give me a break—and a penchant for extended metaphors, like 'taken off the tinsel by putting on the dog'. You don't have to be a lit major to see the progression from 'serenely sebaceous' to 'porcine peony,' either. You know as well as I do, *Andre* wrote that review for *Faded Flowers* . . . and everything else that's come out under Jason Saylin's byline."

Edging toward the door, with his freckles in high relief against the pallor of his skin, Franklin said, "This is a very silly and dangerous game you're playing, Jocelyn, and I don't want any part of it."

"Then how about a round of anagrams," she asked blithely, flipping to the front of the book. "I've seen you at parties. You're great at anagrams, Franklin."

Allen stopped dead in his tracks and whispered, "Anagrams?"

"That's right. Making a new word out of the letters of another, you know. See, the inscription here says, 'To Ainsly—and a new beginning.' On the surface it's a little cryptic, but if you shuffle the letters around you find that 'Ainsly' also spells 'Saylin.' Isn't that cute? As for 'Jason'—that means 'healer,' doesn't it? And 'guérisseur,' in French, means 'healer of time.' It takes forever to figure out, but once you do things become real clear."

"Crystal, I'd say," Phillip interjected, as Allen slumped into a nearby chair. "They each had what the other one lacked—Andre, the mind and the writer's gift; and Ainsly, the 'stage presence.' Separately they might've achieved minor recognition. Together they created the penultimate theatre critic—a man of brilliance and verve. Now, what I'd like to know, Franklin, is which of those three people—Ainsly, Andre or 'Saylin'—offered to put money into *Hedda?*"

"You . . . you have to understand," Allen gasped, looking like a hyperventilating gerbil, "it *wasn't* blackmail. I never meant . . . I had no *proof.* I merely told Drucker what I had guessed. After reading *Lost Ladies* and seeing the first review of *Hedda,* I told him it sounded like Andre grinding an old axe. That's all I said! But the next day I got a letter from his lawyers offering the backing, so I knew I was right. I never, never thought it would lead to all this! I had no idea that he told Andre. You have to believe me, I'm sick about it . . . have been for days. And now it's driven two men to take their own lives when I would never have said a *word—*"

"Is that what you think?" Gerrard broke in. "That this is a double suicide?"

"What else can I think?" he asked hopelessly, burying his head in his hands.

"Franklin, Franklin, listen to me," Jocelyn insisted softly. "This is important. Did anybody else know about Andre and Drucker? Did you tell anyone?"

"Oh, God, no, at least, I didn't mean to," he said, wiping away the sweat that was pouring off his forehead. "But Marc Carson was in my office the day I got the lawyers' letter. He might've got a peek at it while I was busy. He's been acting like he knew something. I don't know whether he said anything to Irene or not, but—"

There was a sharp rap on the door, followed by the appearance of the formidable head nurse, who declared in a voice as starched as her uniform, "Really, lieutenant, it's after visiting hours. You can't expect me to run my ward like a precinct house. What am I to do with these people?!"

"These people are here on official police business and I'll take full responsibility for them, nurse."

"No, not *these* people," she snapped, gesturing around the room. "I mean the people out in the hall. They won't go away!"

Before the nurse could shut the door behind her, in a group act of visceral confirmation Patsy Snell, Courtney Mason and Marc Carson trooped into the room. They were led by an indignant Irene Ingersoll, who averted her gaze from Jocelyn and glowered at Phillip, demanding, "Just what the all-fired hell is going on here?!"

CHAPTER XXVII

When he was seven years old Tommy Zito had been given an illustrated Bible for his first Holy Communion. Some of the more gruesome pictures from the Old Testament had sprung off the page and into his inchoate imagination, giving him nightmares for weeks until his mother finally hid the awful Good Book in the attic. With characteristic resiliency he had forgotten the whole episode until this moment, when the small hospital room was suddenly converted into a living replica of the Tower of Babel. The room reverberated with various echoes of Irene's initial demand.

"Why wasn't I *told* . . ."

". . . you can't imagine the *shock* it gave me!"

". . . kind of disturbance can't be tolerated. This is a *hospital!*" This from the head nurse.

Amidst the bedlam Jocelyn stayed perched on Phillip's bed, jotting something down in her notebook which she tore out and handed to Gerrard. Seeing Zito's helpless expression, she gave him a quick wink, observing, "Kind of like a Greek chorus on speed, huh?" Before he could make a reply, one voice rose above the others; not surprisingly, it was Irene's.

"Keep your starched paws off me," she bellowed at the head nurse who had been making ineffectual attempts to herd her out the door, "you superannuated candy striper or I'll—"

"*Can it,* Ingersoll!" Phillip's voice rolled like thunder above their heads. Jocelyn could have sworn that she heard the windowpanes rattle, while she marveled at his stamina. "Either settle down or I'll have you up for disturbing the peace—mine! Now, would you like to tell me—calmly—just how you got wind of all this?"

Irene, temporarily at a loss for words, regarded Gerrard with a mixture of outrage and admiration while Marc Carson stepped in to fill the breach. "We called Franklin after the show. His . . . uh

. . . houseguest told us that he came here to see Andre. He didn't say much . . . only that there'd been an accident and it involved the police. So, naturally, we were concerned."

"Naturally," Phillip said cryptically before turning his gaze to Patsy and Courtney. "And what about you?"

He didn't have to ask twice. Courtney seemed fully recovered from her afternoon's ordeal, her color was better than it had been in days and her voice was filled with lively exasperation. "Well, really—I should've been the *first* to be notified! After all—"

Patsy Snell placed a restraining hand on her shoulder and said, "The building super called us. Said the police had broken into Jas——, I mean, Andre's apartment . . . thought Courtney should know."

"I see," he said as his eyes traveled slowly around the room. "Since you're all here and since you're all, as Mr. Carson said, 'concerned' in this affair, I think it's only right that I bring you up to date on some—"

"Excuse me," Jocelyn broke in facetiously, "but, if this is going to be a long 'briefing,' we might need refreshments. Can I get anyone anything—coffee, tea . . . Seconals?"

She received looks of disapprobation from everyone except Tommy Zito, who had caught the subtle "go ahead" nod Gerrard had given her. While she blithely cajoled orders out of everyone, Phillip drew her notebook toward him and scrawled a quick note, which he slipped to his sergeant. Before Tommy had a chance to read it, Jocelyn drew her arm through his, saying, "Can you give me a hand, sarge? Oh, and nurse, I need to ask you about something. I've been having this awful itch . . ." With a radiantly entreating smile, she bore them both out of the room.

Twenty-five minutes later, Jocelyn returned with an array of Styrofoam cups and a mollified head nurse in tow. Zito was nowhere to be seen, but Phillip's rapt audience took no notice as he neared the end of his dramatic summary.

"So, you see," he said, holding Andre's encased note in one hand, "*figuratively* speaking, we know Guérisseur's note is the truth. If he and Ainsly made up Jason Saylin, that composite personality was doomed when Andre decided to strike out on his own.

What remains to be seen is the *literal* truth . . . whether Andre really killed Drucker. That we won't know unless he recovers and we're able to interrogate him."

"Well, I'll be blowed," Irene huffed, raking long fingers through her magnificent blond mane. "That rotten first review, with all those nasty cracks, was the work of that whey-faced runt?! And I always thought of him as sort of cosmopolitan Mr. Peepers."

Franklin Allen was sufficiently recovered by this time to mutter, "Typecasting is always a mistake, I think."

"What I don't get," she continued, paying no heed as usual to her director, "is why he came down so hard on me in the 'Saylin's Solution' column? After all, it wasn't *Andre* who ended up with pasta on the lapels."

"That's a moot point, I think," Gerrard said, executing a small wheelie in his chair. "At least as far as the two of them were concerned. Ainsly was the physical embodiment of Jason Saylin in the eyes of the world. When you attacked him, you attacked them both. And written retaliation was Andre's department."

Playing silent butler, Jocelyn dispersed drinks around the room with muted efficiency while mentally congratulating Phillip on a fine performance. The cool authority in his tone left no doubt in her mind that he had missed his true calling. He was a remarkably quick study. Considering how new this supposition was to him, he was "winging it" like an old improv pro. And, so far, his audience was eating it up.

"But *why* would he want to leave," Marc Carson asked with naked amazement. "I mean, he and Jas——, he and Ainsly had a very sweet setup, there. What made him decide to just walk out and blow it?"

"It could be any number of reasons," Phillip countered. "Ego, for one—the desire to be recognized in his own right." Allen groaned at this unintentional pun, but Phillip was on a roll and didn't let it throw him. "Fear, for another—he might have foreseen the possibility of discovery, especially if he knew someone like Franklin had got hold of *Lost Ladies*."

A gravelly voice broke in. "Nope, that won't play. Andre didn't know *who* had Jason's copy. He said so when he was packing to—"

Patsy Snell's mouth clamped shut in a flash but not in time. Gerrard swung his wheelchair around to face her.

"That's right, Patsy, Andre was finishing his packing today . . . An odd pursuit for a man about to kill himself, don't you think? You went to see him after you left your apartment. Why?"

Like the old war-horse she was, Patsy jumped the hurdle without shying. "I wanted to talk to him about Court. Thought it was time he knew about . . . everything. I thought she might need his help."

Before he could ask his next question, Courtney threw back her head and uttered a sound that was half cackle, half rebel yell. *"His* help?! Oh, Patsy, darlin', what a notion! Why, that man wouldn't take the trouble to piss on me, even if I was set on fire in the middle of a desert, don't you know that, girl?"

All the men in the room were, in varying degrees, shocked by this unexpected outburst. All the women, with the exception of the head nurse, were not. Irene and Patsy chalked it up to the effects of drug withdrawal, but Jocelyn knew it for what it was—the "good ol' girl" side of Courtney peeking out from behind her Southern magnolia exterior. Jocelyn also knew how to play into it. Positioning herself at the end of the bed, opposite Courtney's chair, she affected a subtle drawl and a look of wide-eyed amazement and said, "Now, stop your lyin'! I always thought that man was real fond of you."

"Shoot, no. He's just like my Aunt Mamie. The more she can't abide someone, the sweeter she'll be—'til she practically *chokes* you with it, I swear! That's Andre. He was so mad when I stepped in and took Jason away from him that he . . . well, he nearly gave me *diabetes*, that's all I can say." Choking with laughter, she downed the rest of her soft drink and started in on Patsy's, wiping tears of mirth from her eyes. "Y'all have to excuse me. You must think I'm terrible," she said, reverting to a more demure locution, "but I haven't been able to laugh in *so* long, and this is so funny!"

"What's so funny, Courtney," Gerrard asked quietly.

"The idea of Andre writing all Jason's material—as if he could! All they did was invent a name together. Jason did all the rest. Good Lord, I ought to know! And, if what you're sayin' were true, why in the world would Jason have lent that stupid book to Franklin in the first place?!"

Having no answer to that question, Phillip countered with one of his own. "Then why did Jason put money into *Hedda?*"

"Did he? I had no idea," she responded blandly, lighting a fresh cigarette. "But it doesn't surprise me much, knowing Jason. He was very good at compartmentalizing. He never confused theatre with show business."

Something in her inflection jarred Irene's fine-tuned ear. "What a divinely cryptic remark," she purred. "Just what the hell does it mean?"

"It just means—and, please, don't fret yourself, Irene, honey—that, as an actress, you never were Jason's personal cup of tea, you know that. But he wasn't blind, he saw the audience response you were getting. He told me that if *Hedda* moved to Broadway it stood to make a bundle, with or without his blessings. And he was always very supportive of Franklin, so it's no surprise—"

"No surprise that he'd trash me all the way to the bank, is that it? Of all the crummy, despicable . . ."

Like hungry prizefighters, both women were squaring off in the ring. Fortunately the round ended before it got underway when Dr. Hadley walked through the door. "Lieutenant, I thought you should know—Guérisseur's had another seizure! It's under control now. We've got him sedated, but . . . it doesn't look good."

In the stunned silence which followed, Jocelyn's eyes made a rapid tour of inspection, trying to gauge individual reactions. Snell and Carson stared anxiously at their respective charges; both Patsy and Marc had the air, doubly enhanced by their surroundings, of scientists engaged in a volatile experiment. Courtney, the calmer of the two women, blew tiny smoke rings and watched them float toward the ceiling with abstracted absorption while Irene, always aware of her audience, caught Jocelyn's glance and answered it with a look of supreme defiance; only her hands, clinching and unclinching themselves on the armrests, gave her away. The most clearly devastated soul was Franklin Allen, who sat rubbing imaginary grains of sand from his rheumy eyes.

As Marc started gently massaging Irene's ramrod shoulders, Allen jerked his head around to peer up at the tall intern. With a wet cough he asked, "Doctor, if Andre . . . pulls through, when can I . . . when can he have visitors?"

"Not for several days, I'm afraid. Understand, we have to be absolutely certain . . ." Hadley continued, in precise and clinical terms, to give a recap of his earlier discourse on the aftermath of strychnine poisoning and Guérisseur's precarious condition. Enjoying the intentness of his captive audience and seemingly oblivious to their growing discomfort, he wound up by saying, ". . . so, as I'm sure you can appreciate, Mr. Guérisseur has to remain in pretty much total isolation until we're positive that his condition has stabilized."

"That's right," Gerrard interjected. "At this point, Guérisseur is, taking things at face value, our prime suspect. He'll remain here, in unofficial police custody, until it's safe to get a statement from him. That's all I can tell you. We'll try to keep you abreast of the situation but, for now, the ninth floor is strictly off limits."

The note of finality in Phillip's voice left no doubt in anyone's mind that the scene was ending. Snell and Mason led the exodus, followed dejectedly by Franklin Allen. Marc Carson cast a hesitating look in Jocelyn's direction and seemed about to say something, but Irene gave his arm an imperious tug and whisked him away. The good-natured Hadley offered to buy the now completely flummoxed head nurse a cup of coffee.

Left alone with Jocelyn, Phillip gingerly placed a hand on his throbbing ribcage and let out a long suppressed moan. Coming to kneel by his wheelchair, her face a study in concern and perplexity, Jocelyn asked, "Is it bad, love? Are you going to make it all right?"

"Don't worry," he said with an affectionate grin, "I don't feel as bad as you look. What's the matter—having second thoughts?"

"Hell, yes—seconds, thirds and fourths. That didn't play the way I expected," she said, gesturing helplessly in the direction of the departed throng. "Phillip . . . what if I'm *wrong?*"

"We'll know soon enough," he said philosophically. "In the meantime . . ."

"In the meantime, I might've screwed up your whole investigation," she burst out inconsolably, "and you'll have to pay for my—"

"Josh, do me a favor. Just shut up. It's too late for either of us to

go chicken shit on this," he said not unkindly. "We're in this together and it's not going to be pretty. You should know that."

"I know that," she concurred solemnly. "I'm just afraid."

"I know you are," he said, leaning forward awkwardly to kiss her
tenderly on the mouth. "But I also know that, as scared as you are
of being wrong, you're more frightened of being right."

Grasping both his hands tightly in hers, but unable to meet his
searching gaze, she stared down at the linoleum floor and whispered, "Right."

CHAPTER XXVIII

"This old man, he played one. He played knickknack on my thumb. With a . . ." For the tenth time Tony Garvas began crooning the inane ditty that was his six-year-old daughter's current favorite. The innocuous tune had been echoing in his head for days, thanks to his child's awesome capacity for repetition. But for now it was welcomed company, keeping at bay the eerie, suspended hush of the ninth-floor corridor. It was nearly midnight, almost an hour since Lieutenant Gerrard had come up to give him final instructions. The only other conscious body on the ward was the nurse at the night desk, which was at the far end of the hall and out of his line of vision. The sole indication Garvas had of her presence was the faint scratching of her felt-tipped pen, which reminded him, unpleasantly, of mice scurrying across a tenement floor.

Finishing his fourth cup of burned, black coffee, he had the brief sensation of being watched. Not wanting to give play to his fancy, he rose slowly from his chair and executed some of Zito's prescribed relaxation stretches before making a desultory tour of the hallway. Other than the occasional scuff mark, there was nothing to be seen. Satisfied, Garvas returned to his post and charily opened the door of Guérisseur's room. It was very dark inside. What little illumination there was, provided by a small table lamp removed as far as possible from the hospital bed, showed Garvas that the patient was, at least to the naked eye, resting comfortably. Feeling reasonably assured, the policeman checked his watch, saw that he had another hour to go before his relief came and decided to make a quick dash to the men's room.

No sooner had the lavatory door swung shut behind Garvas than a white-smocked figure stole around the near corner of the corridor and made for Guérisseur's room with a purposeful tread. Once inside, there was a frozen pause as the eyes adjusted to the dim lighting and the ears struggled to block out the sound of labored breathing coming from the bed. Then the imperatives of fear and necessity took over with galvanic force.

He was sleeping on his back, head turned toward the wall, but the i.v. was still attached to his right arm. That was the important thing. One hand reached into a pocket to withdraw a small paper packet while the other struggled to disconnect the i.v. tube from the feed bottle, finally succeeding. Fighting the crushing pressure of time, both hands worked to filter the fine white powder into the tubing, careful not to let any particles spill onto the floor. This done, the tube was reattached to the bottle and a long-held breath was released with the force of jet expulsion.

"There, you son of a bitch, I'm done with you—finally! You did everything you could to ruin my life and you succeeded. If it weren't for you, he'd . . . No, I can't think of that. I'll go crazy! The only important thing is that you *rot*, Andre, you rot in hell!"

The hissed notes of hysterical triumph ceased suddenly. Something wasn't right. Something was wrong with the i.v. needle, the way it was strapped to the inert arm. The white-coated figure leaned forward to make a closer examination, extending a reluctant hand toward the defenseless man. Flesh contacted flesh which was no longer quiescent. Suddenly a broad hairy hand grabbed a fine-boned wrist as the body on the bed began to rise ghost-like from beneath the sheets.

Standing in the doorway, Tony Garvas flipped on the ceiling lights, creating a cold fluorescent glare. He felt as if he had just stepped into a grade-B horror film. *The Curse of the Mummy's Tomb* came irresistibly to mind as he beheld Tommy Zito, still encased in bed linens, staring hard into the enormous emerald pinwheels spinning in Courtney Mason's eyes.

"You're not . . . Where's Andre?" she gasped.

"On another floor," Zito said, tentatively relaxing his grip. "Phil had him moved two hours ago."

Both men stayed tensed, waiting for the initial shock to recede and the expected wave of entrapped rage to hit. Her reaction, when it came, however, was both less and more than they had anticipated.

"Why, I declare," she said as a tremor of hysterical laughter shook her slender frame. "That man has more lives than a cat. For a puny runt, he sure is hard to kill 'cause, Lord knows, I've tried . . . I have *tried!*"

CHAPTER XXIX

"Alright, O'Roarke, you got me out of bed at two in the morning, so this had better be good," Patsy Snell barked, striding down the hall of the police station and brusquely pulling up a chair by Tommy Zito's desk. "Where's Court?"

"She's in there," Jocelyn said, giving a weary jerk of her head in the direction of Phillip's office and lighting her tenth consecutive cigarette. Patsy's abrasive manner was a thin-as-ice covering for the nameless dread lurking in her eyes. Jocelyn, whose dread now had a name to it, steeled herself before adding, "She's with her lawyer."

"Lawyer? Why the—Josh, what's going on?"

"She's making a confession. Now, take it easy, Patsy! Nobody's putting the screws to her. It's purely voluntary on her part. In fact, I think it's a relief, really. But when it's over, they'll book her and take her to the detention center and I was afraid . . . well, I thought she might need you with her."

"Book her . . . for what?!"

"For manslaughter. She killed Jason Saylin. Well, that's not accurate. She killed Ainsly Drucker—by accident. She *meant* to kill Andre and she tried to again tonight."

Incipient sounds of protest died in Patsy's throat as the two women exchanged a look which spoke volumes of shared insight. Slumping back in her seat, Patsy let out a heartfelt sigh and said, "So, it's true. Andre really did write all the Saylin reviews and everything?"

"Oh, yes, it's true. I don't think Courtney knew anything about it when she first got involved with Drucker, but once they became engaged and she moved into the penthouse with them everything had to come out into the open. By that point, she was so in love with Drucker and his public persona that it shook her badly when Andre announced his intentions of leaving. It shook Ainsly, too.

That's why he played ball with Franklin. They both tried everything they could think of to change Andre's mind. When nothing worked, Courtney decided that Andre had to die."

"But why . . . if Andre was their golden goose, why would she want him *dead?*"

"To protect Drucker . . . and herself, of course. I think she'd convinced herself that, together, they could sustain the Saylin image. But Andre, off on his own and writing as a free agent, was too much of a threat."

"But he'd never *say* anything. She must've known that! Andre's too loyal."

"That's true. But what if he *wrote* something—anything—and it got published? People in the business might read it, if only out of curiosity, and certain inferences would be made—especially if it coincided with a noticeable decline in Saylin's style. It wouldn't necessarily mean the end of his career but—"

"It would mean the end of his reign," Patsy finished for her, nodding her head with sad and final acceptance. "The end of everything Court wanted from that marriage—prestige, security . . . identity. That's what she wanted more than all the rest. Definition. Oh, God, Josh, it sounds so awful, but you know her! She's vain and self-centered, but she was never just a venal bitch on the make!"

"I know, Patsy, I know," she said soothingly, handing her a lit cigarette and hoping to stem the tide of the older woman's anguish. Jocelyn was too close to her own breaking point to risk watching Gibraltar crumble. "Courtney's always needed to be someone special. Coming from her neck of the woods, that means one thing— being the *wife* of someone special. She might've cared as much about what Ainsley was as who he was, but that doesn't mean she didn't love him. I think she did and that's what's so terrible for her now. She must be in agony."

Taking a sharp draw off her cigarette, Patsy suddenly recovered some of her normal acumen and demanded, "But why . . . if the strychnine was meant for Andre, how did it get into Drucker's cocaine?"

Before Jocelyn could answer, the office door opened and Phillip stepped out into the hallway. Leaning against the door, looking half-dead and badly in need of the wheelchair he had so stubbornly spurned on leaving the hospital, he stared down at the floor with a curious look of pained reluctance. Jocelyn, fighting the urge to leap up and lend him a shoulder to lean on, asked, "Is it over now?"

"Just about. She's made her statement and it's all there. She wants to plead guilty but her lawyer's got 'temporary insanity' written all over his face. But she's made one small request," he said, rubbing the back of his hand across his brow. "Before we take her downstairs, she wants to see—"

Patsy Snell was already out of her chair and halfway to the door. "Of course, I'm ready—"

He halted her progress with a gently restraining hand. "No, sorry, Patsy," he said, finally raising his gaze to give Jocelyn a look of disarmed tenderness and commiseration. "She wants to see *you*."

They were alone in the room, or as good as. The solitary policewoman, who had been assigned as Courtney's guard, contrived with chameleon-like ability to fade back against her surroundings. Jocelyn saw her as soon as she entered Phillip's office, but she made no more impression than the filing cabinet or the cactus on top of it. At that moment nothing short of a flash flood would have; Jocelyn's integral attention was keenly focused on the passive figure sitting beside the desk. Drawing up a chair opposite her, Jocelyn was struck anew by Courtney's loveliness. Drained of all anxiety, possessed of the serenity of the doomed, she gave Jocelyn a smile which, though weary, was filled with reckless charm and a touch of irony. She kept smiling and said nothing, clearly relishing Jocelyn's discomfort and leaving the first move up to her.

"Phillip said you wanted to see me, Court."

"Hmm, yes, I did," she answered dreamily. "I wanted to ask you a few things, Joshie. Just out of curiosity, you know?"

"Well . . . sure. Though I think Phillip's in a better position to tell you what—"

"No! I didn't want to hear it from him. I want to hear it from *you*. He'd just give me the facts . . . list the evidence. And I already know what all that is."

"Oh, I see," Jocelyn lied with quiet conviction. She sensed an oblique purpose underlying Courtney's gentle mien, but she had no clue as to its objective. "I'll tell you whatever I can."

"Fair 'nough. I knew I could count on you . . . to be fair. It's your prime feature—fairness. You've never been real sweet to me, Joshie, but you always let me know where I stood."

"Let you know?! Court, up until last week, we hadn't spoken to each other in nearly a *year!*"

"Oh, but I remember . . . I remember when we did that show together in St. Louis. Don't you?"

"Sure, but that was years ago," Jocelyn replied uneasily. Something in those suddenly avid green eyes told her that Courtney remembered it as if it were yesterday.

"You thought I stunk, didn't you? Course, you never said so flat out and you always covered for me when I went up. But you made it real clear that I wasn't pulling my weight onstage . . . that I was second-rate."

There was no point in denial or appeasement, and they both knew it. Jocelyn sighed, "I thought you were miscast, that's all. It wasn't your fault. Happens all the time."

"But not to *you!* You were playing a middle-age alcoholic and you made it work."

"I knew a lot of tricks and a *lot* of alcoholics. I was lucky."

"What's luck?" Courtney demanded.

"Good question," Jocelyn answered, only slightly dismayed by the philosophical bent their conversation was taking. "Well, my friend, Ruth, who's a great opponent of what she calls 'magic thinking,' says luck is when preparation meets opportunity."

Courtney gave a hiccuping chuckle. "Oh, that's good! I like that. Ruth's right, you know. Everybody said I was a lucky girl when Jason fell in love with me. But I knew it would happen. I *was* prepared for it. I just wasn't prepared . . . for the other."

"For Andre falling in love with you, you mean?"

"Yes—and it spoiled everything. That's what made Andre decide to leave—the fool! Jason knew and he understood. Why did Andre have to ruin it all?!"

Sensing the futility of it, Jocelyn forbore making the obvious answer and waited for Courtney to recommence her arcane agenda. It didn't take long. Staring unseeingly at the Magritte print, Courtney took a deep breath and asked, "How did you know?"

"I didn't—not for certain. It was an educated guess, nothing more," Jocelyn said, adopting straightforward bluntness as the kindest tact. "I thought from the start that Jason's death wasn't an outside job. It involved intimate knowledge of that apartment and its personal effects. That's why I stumped on Andre until . . ."

"Until you read his book. Yes, I see. But did you *know* when we all came into the hospital tonight that it was me?"

Baffled by the urgency in the other woman's voice, Jocelyn shook her head and said, "No, I wasn't sure. But it seemed pretty certain that Jason wasn't the intended victim. That left Andre and his suicide note. If he didn't kill Jason, he knew who did and was trying to cover up for it. If he never made it out of that hospital, no one would ever know for certain whether or not he really killed Drucker, or whether he actually wrote the reviews. We figured that you might want to keep it that way."

"So your lieutenant had Andre moved. That was real sly. I had no—" Courtney stopped in mid sentence as a new thought struck her. She sat bolt upright, grasping both sides of the chair. A look of dawning epiphany lit up her face. "You all arranged the whole thing right *there*, didn't you?! You set it up right under our noses in that room, isn't that right?"

A flush of guilty embarrassment crept up Jocelyn's neck. It felt unnervingly surreal to be explaining to the fly how the spider made the web. "Well, it certainly wasn't rehearsed, if that's what you mean. We were . . . uh . . . more or less playing it by ear."

"And that's why you took the sergeant with you when you went to get drinks?"

"That's right. Phillip had slipped him a note about having Andre moved. I explained the rest and had a word with Hadley."

"That cute young doctor—you coached him?! Then all that stuff about Andre having another seizure was bull ticky?"

Jocelyn gave a feeble nod, then murmured, "He's much better, actually. Looks like he's going to pull through fine."

"Well, if that don't beat all. You know, Joshie, you really *should* be a director. You've got a real knack for staging," Courtney remarked with airy inconsequence. "At least I don't have to feel like a damn fool. I've been done in by real pros."

"You did yourself in, Courtney, and you know it," Jocelyn stormed, suddenly enraged by this pose of rueful martyrdom. "My

God, Andre was ready to die to protect you—and because he knew you'd wanted him *dead!* Phillip had to do what he did because he knew that, even under questioning, Andre wouldn't break if it meant exposing *you!* You didn't have anything to fear from him."

"Oh, *didn't* I? Fat lot you know," Courtney shouted, leaping out of her seat. "Look, I could cope with nice, healthy commercial blackmail. But Andre would never do that—oh, no!—he'd *forgive* me and that's worse . . . that's sick. It's not love, it's obsession! And I'd have to live with it for the rest of my life, especially once he found out—"

Again something stopped her, but this time it was dread, not excitement. A look of pure revulsion flashed across her face. Jocelyn caught it and the final piece of the puzzle clicked into place. Fancy and fact met in a potent fusion, making it difficult for her to speak. "Court . . . the baby? Jason really was sterile, wasn't he? The baby . . . is Andre's?"

Courtney Mason stood in the center of the room, swaying as if stirred by an angry wind. With great effort she anchored herself by focusing on the linoleum floor with leaden eyes. When she finally spoke her voice was thick with disgust. "I told you that I tried *everything* to keep Andre from leaving. Tell me, do they allow abortions in prison?"

When at last Jocelyn emerged from Phillip's office, feeling cold and miserable, Patsy Snell went at her with fretful concern.

"What went on in there?! Jesus—it's been thirty minutes. What did she say?"

Jocelyn shook her head weakly and tried to make words come out, but nothing happened. Phillip, long familiar with the symptoms of empathetic shock, removed Patsy's insistent hand from Jocelyn's elbow and placed a gentle arm around her shoulder.

"It's alright," he whispered. "It doesn't matter now. The worst part is over."

"Doesn't matter," Patsy protested. "Maybe not to you! But I need to know. What did she want, Josh?"

"My critique—that's all," Jocelyn croaked as an awful sensation of uncontrollable giddiness swept over her.

"Critique? What the hell are you talking about," Patsy demanded.

Summoning up her last reserves of will, Jocelyn answered, "The whole scene she played in the hospital. She wanted to know if it was convincing, if I thought . . . if I thought she'd finally learned how to act."

CHAPTER XXX

"Emerson said, 'The reward of a thing well done, is to have done it,'" Frederick Revere remarked, deftly working the cork out of a bottle of Dom Pérignon. "He's right, of course, but that doesn't mean we can't have a few perqs on the side now, does it?"

The cork came out with a lusty pop. With a quick turn of the wrist, Revere poured out three full glasses without spilling a single drop as Jocelyn snuggled back in her chair and sighed with aesthetic appreciation. They had just come from seeing a delightful revival of *You Can't Take It with You* and were cosily sequestered in one of the intimate lounges at the Gardenia Club.

Initially, Jocelyn had been nervous about the evening. It was Frederick's treat, what he called "a thin ploy to obscure my rampant curiosity," and also his first chance to get a look at Phillip Gerrard. All three were aware of the significance of the occasion— Phillip especially, who sensed that it was tantamount to being taken home to "meet the folks." He didn't resent this, knowing Jocelyn's deep attachment to the old actor, and in an elliptical way it fit in nicely with his own plans. He fingered the small velvet box resting in his coat pocket and wondered if the wily silvered-haired gentleman had guessed his intentions.

Jocelyn certainly hadn't, of that he was certain. Effused with the blithe good will that only Kaufman and Hart can engender, she raised her glass and said, "Let's have a toast! What shall we drink to?"

"To the meeting of true minds," Revere asserted as they all clinked glasses. He shot her a mischievous smile, adding, "And thank you for supplying me with a graceful segue, my dear. I am afire to know how your true and clever minds ever came to light on Courtney as the killer?"

"Well, one good douse deserves another," Jocelyn rejoined, holding out her glass for a refill. "And you've certainly earned it, Freddie. You're the one who told me that Franklin had a copy of Andre's book. Once we'd got ahold of that, things sort of tumbled into place—rapidly."

"So I gather. But there's a quantum leap in there somewhere." He fixed Phillip with a pleasant but penetrating look. "How did you figure out that Drucker wasn't the intended victim?"

"Andre's suicide attempt, for one thing. A man who commits a premeditated crime successfully isn't likely to take his own life. Besides, Andre wasn't the one who had something to hide. If it came out that he wrote the reviews, he wouldn't suffer for it. But Drucker would and so would Courtney. They had the biggest investment in keeping it deep and dark. And then, there were the gifts."

"Gifts? What gifts?"

"The matching gifts that Court always gave to the both of them. It was a private joke among the three of them," Jocelyn interjected. "Andre and Ainsly were both 'Saylin,' so Courtney gave them identical gifts—walking canes, sombreros . . . and coke vials."

"Good God! You mean the second vial—the one with the strychnine in it already—that was *Andre's?!* She must've been mad to take such a risk."

"Not really. The odds were heavily on her side," Phillip replied. "Cocaine use was really Drucker's big thing. Andre and Courtney more or less went along for the ride. When Ainsly doled it out, they partook. And with Andre on the brink of moving out, there was very little likelihood that he'd use his private stash until he was well out of the apartment and on his own. Knowing that Andre experimented with strychnine as an aphrodisiac, Courtney got hold of some when they were all down in Mexico. She figured that Andre wouldn't use it until he was out of Manhattan and at his teaching job. By then, chances were good that his death would be regarded as a simple suicide or a kinky-sex fatality, seeing as how the autopsy would be bound to show that he had plenty of strych in his system already."

"I see, I see. How awful," Frederick murmured, his face a somber acknowledgement of desperation and venality. "But why would Drucker . . . How did it go wrong?"

"The shot of accident," Phillip replied, unabashedly pleased to be able to work some Shakespeare back into the conversation. "Drucker was expecting a cocaine delivery that night. It never came. His courier bought it on the Lower East Side earlier in the evening. That was something Courtney couldn't have foreseen, and Ainsly didn't tell her about the missed shipment. He just walked from the study into Andre's bedroom and borrowed the other vial. Ainsly always trusted his luck and he trusted Andre. He had no idea how desperate Courtney was to protect him."

"Hmm, almost as desperate as Guérisseur seems to have been to protect her," Revere observed dryly. "I don't mean to denigrate the unfortunate man but, if masochism were an Olympic event, he'd certainly be a gold medalist. No wonder she confessed. It was her only real way out of the house of bondage, wasn't it?"

"That's what she thought," Jocelyn said, rubbing away the goose bumps that Frederick's all too prescient comment had given her. "But it doesn't look that way. Now that Andre knows she's carrying his child, his devotion—or whatever you want to call it, and I'm sure there must be a clinical term—has redoubled. He's hired a topflight criminal lawyer to defend her. And I'll bet my residual checks he'll be at the trial every day, offering her a hand to hold. You know, I can't help feeling sorry for Courtney. It's like that old proverb—'Be careful what you wish for . . . You may get it.' Courtney's always had an overriding desire to be sheltered by unquestioning love. Between Andre and Patsy, she's got it in spades. It sounds corny, but I don't think the law can punish her more than Fate already has."

"It *is* corny but—what the hell—you're entitled."

The earthy voice coming from behind her brought fresh waves of goose bumps to Jocelyn's arms. With a stomach-churning sense of déjà-vu she jerked round in her seat and looked up into Irene Ingersoll's limpid blue eyes. Irene exchanged a conspiratorial glance with Revere before addressing the party with uncharacteristic meekness.

"Sorry to burst in like this. I just wanted to get something to eat after the show . . . like a nice dish of crow . . . Josh, can I talk to you for a minute?"

The two women withdrew to a dark corner of the lounge while the two men looked on with avid interest. Their voices didn't carry, but Irene's body language, always expressive, spoke volumes of remorse and supplication. When Phillip finally turned back to his companion, he found Revere studying him with a delicate, almost tender, regard.

"What do you think is going on over there?" Phillip asked.

"Oh, the usual, I'd guess—love and business. Actors have a hard time separating the two. For Irene, it's impossible. Jocelyn is unique in knowing where to draw the line and when—But I'm sure you know that."

There was something so ingenuously benign and understanding in the old man's gaze that, before he knew what hit him, Phillip heard himself blurt out, "I want to marry her."

"Yes, I thought you might. It accounts for that irregular bulge in your left pocket. Does Jocelyn know?"

"No. Not yet. There hasn't been time. Even now—well, this whole business has been rough on her. Maybe it's too soon. What do you think?"

"I think that you're quite an exceptional young man. Jocelyn's told me so, of course. But I can see it for myself, now. You can appreciate what's best in her. You both share a sort of moral ruthlessness that's above personal ambition and twice as strong. And you're both, by nature and profession, compulsive problem solvers. If life were simple that would be enough."

"Ah, I thought I felt a 'but' coming. What is it, Frederick?"

"Like most passionate agnostics, Jocelyn has a finical sense of ethics. She feels things deeply, but in matters of the heart she's the antithesis of your friend, Guérisseur . . . and Courtney, too. She's a loyal soul, but she won't do anything that might compromise herself or you. That's not her idea of love."

"Alright, alright. I know all this! What are you driving at?"

"Just this—timing is everything, dear boy, in theatre and in life. Trust me on this. Having been married to an enormously gifted woman, I know whereof I speak."

"And you think the time's not ripe, eh? Why? Because of the Saylin business? We had some bad moments there—she might have told you about that—but that's over now. And Jocelyn's pretty resilient."

"Lord, yes—sturdy as a horse, that girl. And proud as the devil,

I'm afraid. I don't think she'll be able to see her way clear to marrying you until she's sure of her dowry."

"Her *dowry?!*" Phillip gave an incredulous snort. "You mean like two chickens and a goat? Or a cask of ducats? That's archaic!"

"Maybe so, but that's Jocelyn. Appearances to the contrary, she's still at the hand-to-mouth stage of her career, remember. And good notices don't earn interest. That's why she teaches."

"Yes, I know, but why should that make a difference?" Phillip protested, struggling to refute the intuitive logic of Revere's reasoning. "I make enough for both of us."

"That's just it, I'm afraid. I don't mean to suggest any kind of pecuniary competitiveness on her part, nothing of the sort. But, you see, money doesn't mean so much to you or me, because we have enough. For Jocelyn, on the other hand, there's a point of honor involved. As I said, she's proud. She won't come a beggar to the banquet."

Being a man of fierce determination, Gerrard was not easily stymied once he'd set his will toward something. But while the pragmatic, rational side of him wanted to throw Revere's case clear out of court, the instinctive lover heard the ring of truth in the old actor's observations like a death knell. Wistfully he turned to watch Jocelyn give Irene a warm hug before returning, on her own, to the table. Irene went upstairs to the dining room with a happy wave and a wink, while Jocelyn took a long sip of champagne and gazed bemusedly into the distance.

"What was that all about, pray tell? It played a bit long for a standard reconciliation scene," Frederick remarked.

"Yeah, well—color me dumbfounded," she said with a breathy laugh. "When Irene decides to eat crow, she makes a feast of it, that's for sure."

"Vowed to join the Carmelites, has she?"

"Not quite. But she's leaving *Hedda* at the end of June. They want her down at the Arlington Festival to play Amanda in *Private Lives*. She's agreed on one condition . . . that I direct it."

"Well, I'll be blowed," Frederick chuckled. "The woman's a diplomatic genius! She's mended her fences and saved her ass in one fell swoop. Coward's always been your special cup of tea. And I should know, I sat next to you during Liz and Dick's debacle."

"What did you tell her?" Phillip asked.

"That I had to talk to you first," she answered, her eyes filled with trusting hopefulness. "I know you wanted us to go to Maine in June but . . . what do you think?"

Phillip gave her a broad grin as his left hand secretly caressed the small velvet box in a farewell gesture. "I think you'd better give me a set of keys to your apartment . . . so that Angus won't starve while you're away."

Under the table, Jocelyn clasped his now empty hand in happy gratitude as Frederick Revere called for another bottle of champagne.

Since graduating from Ithaca College with a degree in acting and directing, Jane Dentinger has played many roles Off Broadway and in regional theatres. She now lives in Manhattan where she teaches acting and manages Murder Ink, the mystery book store. *First Hit of the Season* is her second novel for the Crime Club.